A Bayou Wedding

Miss Fortune World (A Miss Prim & Proper Mystery), Volume 3

Caroline Mickelson

Published by J&R Fan Fiction, 2018.

This is a work of fiction. Similarities to real people, places, or events are entirely coincidental.

A BAYOU WEDDING

First edition. August 16, 2018.

Copyright © 2018 Caroline Mickelson.

ISBN: 979-8201248888

Written by Caroline Mickelson.

Chapter One

"ARE YOU REALLY GOING to eat all of that?"

Fork halfway to my mouth, I froze. Had I ever been asked a ruder question? I think not. I squared my shoulders and locked my gaze on the person who had been impudent enough to question my appetite. "Yes, I most certainly am."

"By yourself?"

Reluctantly, I lowered my utensil to my plate and settled back against the booth. Francine's hot and fluffy pancakes were going to grow stone cold, right along with the sides of hash browns, sausage links, and bacon slices that smelled nothing short of divine. But I needed to set a few ground rules with my breakfast companion before I ate a single bite. "I hardly think it's polite to comment on how much of any given food a lady consumes in a gentleman's presence."

Trust me when I say that calling Agent Kase Mayeux of the F.B.I. a gentleman was quite a stretch. Granted, I found him attractive in a sort of hulking, tattooed, scary-sexy sort of way, but that was neither here nor there. He wasn't my boyfriend, although he was determined to spend the week pretending that he was. I, in turn, was going to play along. Just for the one week, because I owed him. Big time.

He lifted an eyebrow, the challenge clear in the way he picked up his fork. I grabbed mine and, with a quick parry and thrust, I managed to thwart his attempt to pilfer a bacon slice.

"Touché." He drew his hand back. "I take it that you've fenced."

"In college, yes." I pushed a small plate toward him. "Please help yourself, Agent Mayeux."

"Why don't you start calling me honey?" he asked as he helped himself to my bacon. "Because I'm going to call you darling."

Darling, which he pronounced as "darlin", was a totally over-the-top choice. But then, over-the-top was standard fare in Sinful, Louisiana. I'd only arrived in town a few weeks earlier myself, ostensibly to look up my great-aunt Ida Belle, although my true purpose had been to hide from the Russian Mob that had a hit out on me.

I'd succeeded at connecting with Aunt Ida Belle, but I'd failed at hiding from the goons who were after me. Two dead bodies and a long story later, here I was sitting across from a federal agent who was on suspension from his job because a delusional ex-beauty queen named Fortune had drugged him while he was on duty so that we could sneak away to rescue my prized Persian cat from a mob boss who was hiding on an island with a stench so horrendous the locals had named it Number Two.

See what I mean? Nothing in Sinful is ever simple.

"Why didn't you order your own breakfast?"

He waved a hand toward the food-laden plates in front of me. "When I heard all that you were ordering, I assumed you were ordering for us both."

"Well, you assumed wrong, Agent Mayeux."

"Not Agent Mayeux," he corrected me. "Honey."

I eyed him warily. "I don't think I can call you that."

"Sure you can, darlin!" His eyes sparkled. "Just try it. You'll like how the word feels as it rolls off your tongue."

My, how he was enjoying this. I, however, felt like I was drowning in quicksand. I had no idea what kind of life Agent Mayeux lived when he was in New Orleans, but my life back in Boston hadn't involved dalliances with men of his ilk. Known around my hometown as the syndicated columnist Miss Prim and Proper, I, Stephanie St. James, was used to dating men who wore a suit and tie to the office. Agent Mayeux, on the other hand, generally sported a black t-shirt, form-fitting blue jeans, shoulder-length black hair worn back in a low ponytail, and a snake tattoo that started at his wrist, traveled up his arm, and wound around his neck. It might well be only an ink snake, but it still unnerved me.

We were hardly what I'd call simpatico. And yet we were going to spend the week pretending to be dating so that he could have a reason to stick around town while he was trying to get information on suspected drug traffickers in the area. I was his cover. But that didn't mean he got to automatically be my honey.

"Are you two going to stare into each other's eyes all day or are you actually going to eat something?"

Startled, I looked up. Francine, the owner of the diner we sat in, stood beside our booth with a pot of coffee in her hand. I hadn't heard her approach, but I was happy to see the steam rising off the coffee pot. With a grateful smile, I pushed my cup toward her.

"Francine, do you think you could please whip up another stack of pancakes here for my girlfriend?" Kase asked. "I'm afraid I've distracted her from eating them while they were hot. And would you please put breakfast on my tab?"

"Young love." Francine rolled her eyes in mock exasperation, but she winked at me as she walked away.

Surprised, I turned back to my companion. "You know, I think she might have actually believed you. About us dating, I mean."

His answering smile was smug. "What's not to believe? You're a beautiful young woman. Stands to reason I'd be attracted to you."

To my horror, I blushed. "This isn't going to work."

Agent Mayeux grinned. "You just said Francine bought it, so I'd say it already is working."

Before I could protest, he slid out of the booth and came around to sit beside me. He laid a possessive arm around my shoulders and leaned down to whisper in my ear. "Don't turn around, but your aunt and her friends are headed this way."

My stomach sank. Aunt Ida Belle was one shrewd woman. She was never going to buy this act. Her best friend Gertie might, because her imagination was like a runaway train. But the third member of their clique most certainly wouldn't. Sandy Sue Morrow, whom everyone called Fortune, was a study in contradictions. She was also smart. Street smart. And she wasn't likely to believe the story that Kase Mayeux was peddling.

Gertie reached our booth first. She looked between Kase and me, which didn't take her long because there was technically no physical space between us. I could feel the warmth of my faux boyfriend's thigh pressed up against my leg.

A wide grin stretched across her wrinkled face. "Well, lookey here. Don't you two love birds beat all?" She slid in across from us. "Tell us how lightning struck."

I turned to my great-aunt. "Aunt Ida Belle, what is she talking about?"

Aunt Ida Belle waved her hand dismissively as she settled in beside Gertie. "Heck if I know. I doubt she even knows what she's yattering about half the time."

Fortune took a chair from a nearby table, turned it to face backward at the end of the booth, and straddled it. I sincerely doubted this was something that she'd learned on the beauty pageant circuit, but I kept my mouth shut. It was hardly polite to mention that she was sitting like a long-distance trucker. Besides, it appeared that Fortune could do no wrong in my great-aunt's and Gertie's eyes. But to my mind, the jury was still out on her.

Agent Mayeux gave my shoulders a gentle squeeze. "I think she's asking what's going on between us." He leaned down and brushed an ever-so-light kiss across my cheek. "Go ahead, darlin', tell them."

Tell them what? That he'd drunk the Sinful Kool-Aid and was now acting as crazy as everyone else in town? Why bother? I was outnumbered. And the inconvenient truth of it all was that I owed him this for my part in humiliating him in front of his co-workers and superiors. I'd have to play along. It was the only polite thing to do under these very bizarre circumstances.

"Kase was kind enough to bring Priscilla back to me yesterday," I paused and gave them all a moment to nod while my mind frantically searched for something to explain this charade. "Well, he asked if I would attend a wedding with him this weekend. And I said yes."

The three women glanced at each other, but before anyone could ask how a wedding invitation led to us sit so indecently close to each other, Francine arrived with yet another stack of piping hot pancakes. Fortunately, their tantalizing aroma distracted my tablemates away from the conversation about my love life and toward what they were going to order for breakfast.

My reprieve, however, was short-lived. Immediately after we were all finished with breakfast, Gertie returned to her earlier line of questioning with the intensity of a small dog gnawing on a very big bone. "Come on, Stephanie, tell us how you and the good agent here got it on without us knowing anything about it."

I dabbed the corner of my lips with a paper napkin. "I hardly think that 'got it on' is an apt description."

Aunt Ida Belle set her coffee mug down and met my gaze. "Perhaps not, but Agent Mayeux here seems to have gone from zero to hero in your eyes in a rather short amount of time. You don't expect us to believe that you've become romantically involved simply because he returned your cat, do you?"

"Rescued and returned." I glanced up at the man in question, but his only reaction was to smile again. Seriously? I hoped my irritation wasn't too obvious. The gentlemanly thing for him to do would be to ride into the conversation and rescue *me*. But it appeared I was on my own. "That's a part of it, of course," I hedged. "Sometimes it's hard to explain how the heart and mind make the choices they do."

Fortune, who had been quiet throughout much of the meal, looked from Agent Mayeux to me and then back. "Who is getting married?"

I was curious myself because I hadn't gotten as far as asking yet.

"The bride's name is Cassandra Masters," he said. "She and her family hail from New Orleans, but her grandmother lives here in Sinful. Apparently, she's lived here all her life. You might know her, name's Lenora Masters."

Ida Belle's eyebrows rose and Gertie's jaw dropped.

"So, you do know her?" I asked.

My great-aunt and Gertie exchanged a quick but telling glance. At the very least, they knew of her.

"Sure, we know Lenora," Aunt Ida Belle finally replied. "Gertie and I went to school with her, all the way from elementary straight through high school."

"The woman's a nut job." Gertie shook her head. "She's been living as a recluse for the last thirty something years, so we haven't actually seen her in the flesh for decades. She never comes into town. Whatever she needs, Walter delivers it to her."

"And you say she's hosting her granddaughter's wedding?" A tiny frown settled between Aunt Ida Belle's eyebrows. "Here in Sinful? Something's not right about that."

Gertie nodded her agreement. "I'm with Ida Belle. Someone's got either the names or facts mixed up. Lenora never had any children, so she can't be a grandmother."

"Hold up a minute, Gertie. Technically she's a step-grandmother," Aunt Ida Belle corrected her. "Don't you remember that her late husband Albert had two sons by his first wife? I don't recall that they ever set foot in Sinful, though. I've just heard tell of them." She turned to Agent Mayeux. "You got the invitation on you, by chance?"

"Sure do." He pulled the invitation out of his back pocket. As he leaned toward me, I caught the scent of fresh pine and soap. I kept my eyes focused on the empty plate in front of me. Regardless of how traitorous my visceral reaction to Agent Mayeux was, there was no need for me to display it for everyone to see. A lady was entitled to her secrets.

He handed a folded card to my aunt. The invitation was printed on cream-colored heavy stock. I watched as Aunt Ida Belle scanned it. Without saying a word, she handed it to Gertie, who glanced at it before handing it to Fortune, who did the same.

"Something's off," Fortune said as she handed it to me.

I took a turn glancing over the invitation, nodding as I returned it to Agent Mayeux. "Yes, there's something very wrong indeed. They chose a serif font."

"Huh?" Gertie frowned. "Where did it say sheriff?"

"No, not sheriff," I hastened to correct her. "Serif. It's a type of a font. It's rather an unconventional choice for a wedding invitation. Back east, brides usually prefer a more traditional sans serif font."

"Sand sheriff? Well, I'll be." Gertie sat back against the booth. "Boston must be a more interesting place than I've been led to believe."

Fortune held up her hand to forestall the explanation she knew I felt was necessary. "Just let it go, Stephanie. We're better off keeping the conversation on track."

No easy thing to do with Gertie.

Aunt Ida Belle spoke next, and her attention was directed to the man next to me. "You're asking a lot for us to believe that you just happened to receive an invitation to a wedding here in Sinful thrown by a social recluse for a step-granddaughter that no one has ever met." She pushed the invitation a bit closer toward his empty plate. "You're going to have to do better than that if you want to include my great-niece in whatever it is you're up to."

I shifted in my seat, uncomfortable with how close Aunt Ida Belle was getting to the truth. But I kept my mouth shut. This was Agent Mayeux's lie to tell, not mine.

"With all due respect, ma'am," he said, his eyes locked on to Aunt Ida Belle's, "there seems to be a misunderstanding. I was invited to this wedding along with a guest of my choice. Your niece was kind enough to agree to be my date. End of story."

Aunt Ida Belle sat back and folded her arms across her chest. Gertie did the same. We all looked at Fortune. She leaned forward.

"The smart thing to do would be to let us in on this from the beginning."

"You're way off base, Fortune." His words held a hint of something I couldn't identify. A warning? A threat?

"Is anyone going to tell me what this is all about?" I finally demanded.

"It's our turf, Mayeux," Aunt Ida Belle said, ignoring me completely.

"We've got connections," Gertie chimed in. "If something in Sinful is going on, we know about it."

"There's no reason to go rogue," Fortune said

"That's rich coming from you," he scoffed.

We sat in an uncomfortable silence for several minutes. I wondered if Fortune felt guilty for lacing Agent Mayeux's milk with a sleeping draught. I cast a curious glance her way, but her expression was difficult to decipher. It certainly didn't say "guilty".

"As charming as it's been to breakfast with you ladies, Stephanie and I have plans for the rest of the day." Agent Mayeux slid out of the booth and helped me to my feet. He opened his wallet and tossed several twenties on the table. "My treat." And then he took hold of my hand and half-dragged me out of Francine's before I could do more than wave goodbye.

Once we were outside of the diner, I put an end to his hustling routine by refusing to take another step. "Just a moment, Agent Mayeux, if you please. Why on earth did we just bolt out of there like that?"

He let go of my hand just long enough to catch my face between his hands. My eyes widened as he lowered his lips to mine and kissed me. Kissed me, Stephanie St. James, right in public for anyone to see. I don't approve of public displays of affection unless they're between a parent and child. Or long-lost friends. Or relatives who haven't seen each other in ages. All of these thoughts raced through my mind as my companion kissed me. I suppose I could have pushed him away, but that would have been rude. So very rude.

"Honey, remember?" he whispered when he lifted his head, his eyes not leaving mine. "You've got to quit calling me Agent Mayeux. You're going to blow our cover."

Breathless, I stared up at him.

"There, that ought to help convince them. Don't look back, because they're watching." He put his hand on my lower back and gently directed me towards his waiting pickup truck. "Carter warned me about those three," he said as he pulled out onto Main Street. "We're going to have to move fast."

Personally, I'd say that we were moving plenty fast. I hadn't known this man more than a week, and he'd just kissed me like we were lovers standing on a moonlit bridge in Paris. I sat in silence as we drove out of Sinful, and then it occurred to me that I had no idea where we were going. "You're going the wrong way if you were intending to take me back to Aunt Ida Belle's."

"That's not where we're headed." He glanced sideways at me, his expression thoughtful. "There's been a change of plans."

"Care to clue me in?"

He shook his head. "Not really. Why don't you just play along?"

Playing along wasn't very simple when I had no idea what game we were playing. Nothing this morning had made much sense to me. But what did I expect?

I was in Sinful, Louisiana.

Confusion Capital of the World.

Chapter Two

DESPITE MY BEST EFFORTS to find out where we were headed, Agent Mayeux refused to divulge any information. I'd just about given up trying to get anything out of him when he pulled up in front of a set of wrought iron gates that were barely visible due to the green vines growing over them. He lowered his window, swept aside some foliage, and reached out to push a half-hidden buzzer. Wherever we were, he'd obviously been here before.

"Might I know where we are?" I tried again.

In answer, he held up a single finger and pressed the buzzer.

Within seconds, the sound of crackling filled the air. "Go away," a querulous voice intoned just before we heard a dial tone.

My eyebrows rose. Hardly a sterling example of southern hospitality.

Agent Mayeux pushed the button several more times before we heard the static sounds again. "Miss Prim and Proper is here," he announced before the disgruntled voice could order us to leave again.

"Well, why didn't you just say so?" This time the annoyance was mixed with what sounded like a tinge of curiosity. "Who are you?"

"Her bodyguard." He shot me a quick wink. "Miss St. James' schedule is tight this afternoon, so if you'd like to see her, you'd best let us in."

Bodyguard? What was he up to?

The gates swung open with a loud groan. Agent Mayeux wasted no time entering the property. He drove along a winding drive with low-hanging Cyprus trees. I glanced sideways at his profile. He appeared completely at ease.

"Agent Mayeux, I'm going to have to insist that you tell me where we are. If you've just announced that I'm here, surely I should be filled in. What part should I play?"

"That's the beauty of it. You get to be yourself, as prim and proper as you like. My only advice is to stay calm, collected, courteous, and curious."

"Oh, is that all?" I looked out the window and gasped. As if by magic, a two-story white plantation style mansion had materialized from amidst the greenery. However, unlike the front gates, nothing about the house said "overgrown" or "un-manicured". Quite the opposite. The building in front of me could easily have been featured on the cover of *Southern Living Magazine*. I turned back to my companion. "Why would I need a bodyguard?"

"Bodyguard slash boyfriend." Kase twisted in his seat to face me. "Okay, so here's what's going down. You're here in a professional capacity."

"As Miss Prim and Proper?"

"Exactly. The key is to keep the focus on you and off of me. It'll compromise the investigation if anyone catches on that I'm a federal agent. Questions?"

A dozen, easily, but I'd start with the most pressing. "If no one in the Masters family knows who you are, how did you manage to wrangle an invitation to the wedding?"

His lips lifted in his trademark half-smile. "Technically, I haven't been invited."

That made about as much sense as Gertie's penchant for fishnet stockings. "But I saw the invitation at the diner. Was it a fake?"

"No, it was genuine all right. But it was your invitation, not mine."

"Mine?" I rubbed my temples. Conversations in Sinful were akin to riding a merry-go-round. "But I'd never heard of these people until an hour ago."

"Ah, but they've heard of you, and that's what ultimately matters. When I put out feelers saying that you'd covet an invitation to the wedding, the bride was ecstatic. Apparently, the idea of a society reporter from a big East Coast newspaper gave her quite the thrill."

"But I'm not a reporter, I'm a columnist," I protested. "I've never covered a society event."

"There's a first time for everything." Before I could further object to the role I'd just been cast in, Agent Mayeux slipped out of the truck and came around to the passenger side door. He yanked it open and motioned for me to get out. "Let's roll."

I was tempted to flat out refuse, but why bother? I alighted and turned around to check my reflection in the window. Miss Prim and Proper needed to look put together. Disheveled was just not a good look on me. And then a question popped into my mind. I whirled back around. "Why would a society reporter need a bodyguard?"

I don't know if Agent Mayeux intended to answer that question or not because a series of explosions tore through the air. Before my mind fully registered what I was hearing, he flattened me against the cab of his truck, his body completely covering mine. "Don't move," he hissed in my ear.

He needn't have worried. I was perfectly fine with him being my human shield.

Within seconds he managed to open the truck door and shove me inside. "Get down and stay down until I tell you to move," he barked as if it were the first day of Marine Corp basic training. He slammed the door shut and locked it before I could respond, not that I knew what to say under the circumstances. Being greeted by gunfire was another Sinful first, at least for me.

It wasn't more than a few moments before the door opened again and Agent Mayeux slipped his hand under my elbow to help me out. If there was a graceful way to remove myself from the floor of a pickup truck, I wasn't aware of it. But I did my best. Once I had both feet on the ground, I smoothed my hair back. "What was all that?"

"Fireworks."

My eyebrows rose, but I didn't ask further questions. "Do I look acceptable?"

Agent Mayeux stared down at me, an unreadable expression on his face. "You'll do," he said, his voice just above a whisper. "We've got company behind me. It's show time."

I tried to peer over his shoulder, but of course I couldn't because he was far too massive. "Friend or foe?"

"They're drug dealers. Connect the dots," he whispered. "Are you ready?"

Ready to hop back in the truck and flee, yes. But my stubborn pride was out to get me today. I nodded.

We were shown into the sitting room by a butler who gave us a disapproving onceover that made me question his training. In contrast, his employer greeted me with what appeared to be genuine warmth, although it didn't extend to my companion. She ignored Kase as if he wasn't filling up and overflowing from the dainty damask covered chair he'd settled into.

Our hostess, Lenora Masters, was the absolute picture of a southern belle who had aged with dignity and style. She was several inches shorter than I, which put her at just over five feet tall. Her silver-white hair was pulled back in a sleek chignon, and tasteful pearl earrings adorned her ear lobes, complimenting the triple strand of pearls around her neck.

"My granddaughter Cassandra was over the moon when I told her that you'd graciously offered to feature her wedding in your newspaper's society column."

I shot an annoyed look at my companion. Offered, my eye teeth. I'd been roped into this like an innocent little calf at its first rodeo. I returned my attention to our hostess. "You should know, Mrs. Masters, that weddings are not usually something that I cover."

Our hostess smiled genially. "We're honored to be your first then. This will be the most impressive wedding that Sinful has ever seen."

My mind scrambled for a response. I doubted that I should just come right out and ask, "So, which member of your dysfunctional family is running drugs?" Agent Mayeux should have given me something to work with, for heaven's sake. "I'd love to hear all the details."

"First things first." She held up a china teapot hand-painted with tiny yellow roses. "May I offer you a cup of tea, my dear?"

"Please." I watched in silence as she filled two teacups, one for herself and one for me. I gave Agent Mayeux a pointed glance, hoping that she'd take the hint and offer him a refreshment, but she ignored him as if he weren't in the room. How anyone could do so,

I couldn't imagine. He wasn't the kind of person who was easy to ignore.

"I know Cassandra is ever so eager to share all of her plans for her special day with you, Miss St. James, so I'll let her do the honors."

"Call me Stephanie, please," I said. "Is Cassandra here now?"

"No, she and her mother spent the day in New Orleans meeting with the florist." Lenora Masters shook her head ruefully. "The only person in this world I detest more than my step-son Donny's spineless first wife, Kitty, is the Colombian whore he's married to now. She's such a bitch."

It took everything I had to not spew my mouthful of hot tea all over at her choice of words. Instead, I simply stared, hoping that my expression didn't reflect my horror. Before my very eyes, sweet, genteel Lenora Masters had morphed into a foul-mouthed harpy. Who talked about their family like that? In front of strangers?

"Really, she is, you have my word," Lenora hastened to assure me, obviously mistaking my startled expression for disbelief. She leaned forward as if she were about to divulge an old family recipe for Lady Fingers. "Carmen has an eye-popping set of knockers, which explains how she convinced Donny to leave Kitty, but I refuse to believe they're real."

"I see," I managed to choke out, although the only thing I clearly saw was a woman who should be committed. Time to steer the conversation away from Carmen's bustline. "Which other family members will be at the wedding?"

"The majority of our out of town guests are the groom's family. Devon comes from a very well-heeled old family from Virginia. He's a great catch, our Cassandra did a good job getting her claws into him."

Claws? I set my teacup down and took a deep breath.

"Are you all right, Stephanie?" Lenora furrowed her brow. "Has your tea grown cold?"

I shook my head. "Not at all." I glanced over my shoulder but my "bodyguard" was busy looking out the window. Which left me alone in this verbal nightmare of a conversation. I desperately wished it were time to leave, but nothing about Agent Mayeux's body language indicated we were going anywhere anytime soon. Curse him. "Does Cassandra have any siblings?"

Lenora's eyebrows rose. "If you count a worthless, good for nothing, lazy young man who refuses to get a real job, then yes she does. His name is Shawn."

"Shawn," I repeated as if I were trying to commit the name to memory. Truthfully, I just couldn't think of anything else to say. "Tell me about him."

"What's to tell? He smokes pot, wears too much leather, and is hanging around waiting for me to die so he can get ahold of my money." Her sigh was wistful. "Young men were so different in my day."

While Lenora paused to nibble on a scone, I glanced over my shoulder at Agent Mayeux in the hopes he would see that I needed rescuing. But he didn't meet my eye. I followed his gaze but couldn't see anything that would explain his rapt attention.

He stood up. "You ladies will pardon me if I step outside to have a smoke?" While his words were couched in the form of a question, he didn't wait for an answer.

As soon as the door closed behind him, Lenora's eyes narrowed. "I hope that man is not accompanying you to the wedding." She shuddered. "I would prefer to see you with someone far more refined."

I reached up to touch my strand of pearls. There was no way that I would attend the wedding without Kase by my side. Time for yet another change of subject. "Mrs. Masters, I believe you know my great-aunt. Like yourself, she's a life-long Sinful resident."

A delighted smile illuminated her face. "Really? What a lovely surprise. I'd love to meet her." She set her saucer on the table and clasped her hands together. "Why, you must invite her to the wedding. What's her name?"

"Ida Belle."

"Ida Belle?" Lenora's smile faded. "You're related to that unholy bitch?"

Chapter Three

I SIMPLY STARED IN response. How would one even begin to respond to such an uncouth question?

"Still as charming as you always were, huh, Lenora?"

I knew that voice. I was related to that voice. I whirled around to find my great-aunt standing in the doorway. "Aunt Ida Belle, what on earth are you doing here?"

"Poaching," Lenora snapped before Aunt Ida Belle could answer. "Same as she's always done. The woman never could keep her hands off my property."

My great-aunt snorted. "Property? That's rich."

"Obviously you ladies have a history." I looked between them. Aunt Ida Belle and Lenora had their gazes locked on each other. "Perhaps we should leave?"

"Fine with me," she said. "Unless Lenora wants to hash this out once and for all?"

I had no idea what the issue between them was, but I had no interest in staying around long enough to find out.

"You can go and never come back for all I care," Lenora spat at my great-aunt.

"Fine," Aunt Ida Belle spat back.

"Fine." Lenora crossed her arms over her chest.

I couldn't remember ever feeling more miserable in my life. Ever. The only saving grace for which I could be thankful was that Gertie was nowhere around. I slipped a hand under Aunt Ida Belle's elbow and closed my fingers around it. I didn't fool myself that I could hold onto her if she decided to lunge for Lenora Masters' throat, but I was hoping she'd take my subtle hint that we needed to be gone.

I turned my attention to our hostess. I had to say something to keep the door of communication open. After all, Agent Mayeux needed access to the Masters family. "Mrs. Masters, thank you for inviting me to tea. I would like to think that this rather unfortunate incident won't preclude us meeting again?"

Lenora tore her gaze from my great-aunt. Her scowl morphed into a refined smile. "Of course not, my dear. I'd love to see you again. Every family tree has a rotten limb." She cast a disparaging look at Aunt Ida Belle. "I don't hold yours against you."

"Thank you." I tightened my hold on Ida Belle's elbow. I didn't need her going off like a loose cannon when I was so close to extricating us from an excruciatingly awkward situation. As I turned to leave, my gaze swept through the room. Everything was in perfect order. Except for the fact that just outside of the large window overlooking the back yard, a pair of legs dangled from the balcony above.

My eyes widened as I zeroed in on the dangler's fishnet stockings. I stifled a groan.

Gertie strikes again.

By the way her legs were swinging wildly, it didn't look like she was going to hold on much longer. We needed to get out of here.

I released my hold on my great-aunt's elbow and draped my arm around Lenora's shoulders instead. I tried to gently angle her so that she wouldn't be able to look out the window. Aunt Ida Belle's sharp intake of breath told me that she'd seen Gertie. Seen her? She'd no doubt put Gertie up to this.

"Where's your unsavory companion?" Lenora asked.

It took me several seconds to realize that she was referring to Kase, not Gertie. And it was a valid question. Where was my bodyguard?

"I imagine he's waiting outside. We should definitely be going," I said, stating the obvious. "Isn't that right, Aunt Ida Belle?"

"Where's my wedding invitation?" she demanded. "It must have gotten lost in the mail."

Lenora's face flushed a deep red. "The only thing that should get lost is you, you old prune."

Out of the corner of my eye, I could still see Gertie's legs. While Gertie's spirit was strong, I doubted her bones were. Heaven only knew what she was going to fracture if we didn't get her down.

"Aunt Ida Belle, why don't you go on ahead? I'd like a word with Mrs. Masters." I could only hope she'd find a way to rescue Gertie. The one thing I didn't doubt was that the two of them had plenty of experience getting each other out of ridiculously precarious positions over the years.

But before she could say a word, a fit and toned blonde streak caught my eye as it raced toward Gertie. Fortune to the rescue. I knew I shouldn't, but I couldn't stop staring. Luckily, Lenora was too busy glaring at my great-aunt to notice that I was agitated.

"I'm not going anywhere until this old biddy invites me to the wedding." Aunt Ida Belle's voice brooked no argument. Fine, she wouldn't get one from me. We could stand here and argue while Fortune rescued Gertie.

"Like hell I will, Ida Belle." Lenora's face had grown increasingly red. I prayed it was her temper flaring and not a stroke coming on. "You're no more welcome here than the plague is."

"I'll bring Walter as my date."

I shot a surprised look at Aunt Ida Belle. Walter? What did he have to do with anything?

Apparently quite a bit, because the mention of his name sent Lenora straight for my aunt's throat. Aunt Ida Belle went for Lenora in a tit for tat move. And I let her. If these two women, who together had more than a century and a half of life experience, wanted to act like mud wrestlers, so be it.

"You'll pardon me, won't you?" I called over my shoulder as I made a dash for the doorway. Neither woman answered, but whether this was for a lack of caring or a lack of oxygen, I wasn't certain. I ran out the front door, around the front of the house, toward the back lawn. By the time I got there, I found Fortune struggling with Gertie.

"Just let go, for God's sake." Fortune's uplifted arms were wrapped around Gertie's knees. "I've got you."

"Not going to happen, sister. I can pull myself up."

"No, you can't. Just let go."

I came to a halt and put my hands on my hips. A more ridiculous spectacle than this, I couldn't imagine. "Do as she says, Gertie," I called out. "This instant. Aunt Ida Belle needs our help."

"I vote you just leave her there," a male voice said from behind me.

I whirled around, unaware that we'd been joined. A twenty-something-year-old young man sporting long brown hair and tighter-than-tight black leather pants stood just behind me, his arms crossed over his chest. This must be Cassandra's ne'er-do-well brother, Shawn.

"She's old," he continued, his voice surprisingly languid considering the circumstances. "I doubt she's got enough muscle tone to hold on for long." He shifted his attention from a struggling

Gertie and gave me a once-over, twice. "And who might you be, toots?"

Toots? Who talked like this? "Mind your manners, young man." I didn't care how pompous I sounded. Disrespecting women was a hot-button issue with me. I pointed toward a wiggling Gertie and a struggling Fortune. "The gentlemanly thing to do would be to assist these ladies."

He shrugged. "Sure thing." He sauntered over to stand behind Fortune. But instead of reaching out toward Gertie, he pinched Fortune's bum.

I gasped. Gertie bleated in surprise when Fortune let go of her. But neither of our shocked expressions held a candle to Shawn's guttural cry when Fortune's roundhouse kick knocked him to the ground. Before Shawn could do more than swear, Fortune dropped to her knees, flipped him into a prone position, and had his arms twisted behind him in what looked like an excruciatingly painful manner.

"You got a death wish, punk?" Fortune ground out through a clenched jaw. "Cause if you do, I can be your fairy flippin' godmother and make it come true. Just say the word."

"I like a chick with attitude," Shawn was unwise enough to say.

Fortune twisted his arms into an even more uncomfortable position, judging by his sharp intake of breath. "Touch me again and you'll eat dirt, got it?"

"Help?" Gertie's warbling voice brought my attention straight back to her precarious position.

I hurried over and wrapped my arms around her knees. "It's okay, you can let go," I lied. Of course, it wasn't okay because we'd topple to the ground together in a messy heap the minute she released her hold, but it wasn't like she could hold on forever. "Just do it, Gertie. On three. One, two..." but before I got to three, a brawny set of arms encircled me.

"Three." Kase finished the countdown for me.

Gertie did as she was told, no small thing considering her rogue tendencies. Kase's arms caught her and his body cushioned us so that we collectively only took a small step backward rather than tumbling to the ground. "Steady, ladies?"

Gertie stepped away first and shook herself off. "I'm still in fighting form."

Kase didn't release his hold on me. "You okay, darlin'?"

"I am, thank you." And I was, unless one counted my breathlessness and thundering heartbeat – neither of which could be blamed on Gertie's escapade. I moved back to put some much-needed space between us.

But he closed the space in one neat step and lowered his head to whisper so that only I could hear him. "What the hell are your friends doing here?"

"How should I know? I don't even know what I'm doing here." My eyes narrowed. "Where have you been?"

"Missed me, did you?" He didn't even try to hide his amusement.

I had. And the thought irked me. Badly. "I certainly don't appreciate being abandoned." I tore my gaze from his and nodded in the direction of Fortune, who was still straddling Cassandra's brother. "Perhaps you might assist Fortune now?"

He snorted. "Looks to me like she's got the situation under control."

Under control? "She's likely to break at least one of his arms if we don't stop her."

"Well, now, that oughta teach him not to touch a woman without permission, don't you think?"

"You tell 'em." Gertie sounded downright delighted. My, but she recovered quickly.

I strode over to Fortune. "I highly recommend you resist the temptation to break his bones." Really, this needed to be said? "Let's go. Aunt Ida Belle might need rescuing. Or maybe Mrs. Masters will instead. Either way, we need to join them before someone gets hurt."

The gunshot that followed my words proved my concern was valid.

Chapter Four

AGENT MAYEUX, GERTIE, Fortune and I raced toward the front door. Shawn stuck close to Fortune like some sort of leathery shadow. One right after the other, we burst into the foyer.

"Who discharged a weapon?" Kase demanded. He held out an arm to restrain Gertie from rushing in to the melee. "Is anyone hurt?"

Lenora Masters whirled around. "Hurt? Yes, you fool, someone has been hurt. I've been wounded. Grievously."

I didn't see a drop of blood anywhere. "Shall I call 911?" I asked.

Aunt Ida Belle harrumphed. "Don't waste your breath. The only thing hurt is her precious ego." The look of disgust on my great-aunt's face left us all with no doubt as to her opinion on the subject of Lenora's feelings.

"We heard a gunshot," Kase persisted. "Where's the weapon?"

Aunt Ida Belle held up her hands to indicate that it wasn't she who fired it. Lenora's hands were clasped together in front of her as if she were posing for a presidential library portrait. Collectively, we turned to look at the three other women who stood in the foyer.

"It wasn't me," a frightened-looking woman said. She wore a pale yellow floral dress and clutched a straw bag in front of her as if it were a shield. Her hands shook as she stared at us. I assumed that this was Kitty, aka the ex-Mrs. Donny Masters, the "spineless first wife".

"Of course, it wasn't you. You're too special—" the last word came out as "es-special" in a thick South American accent, "—to know how to fire a gun." The woman's accented English and ample display of cleavage tipped me off that this was the second Mrs. Masters. Donny's two wives were as classic an illustration of country mouse vs. city mouse as I'd ever seen. "Ha. In my country, women are taught to protect themselves." This proclamation was delivered with a scathing look and a toss of her long dark hair over her shoulder.

I knew who the third woman was before she spoke. Tanned and blonde, everything about her polished appearance said "put-together young professional". My other clue was the *Southern Brides* magazine she held clutched to her chest. This had to be Cassandra, the bride-to-be.

"Miss St. James?" She directed a warm smile in my direction. "Oh, it's such a pleasure to meet you. I can hardly believe you're actually here!" Her reverent tone matched her flattering words. "I'm such a fan of yours."

My intent was to graciously return her kind greeting, but Agent Mayeux had other ideas. "Ya'all have thirty seconds to tell me who fired that shot or I'm calling the cops."

"It was nothing," Lenora said. She waved a dismissive hand toward the front door. "I simply instructed my groundskeeper to take a pot shot at a mangy beast I thought I saw in the yard." She cast a disparaging look at my great-aunt. "Simply to frighten it off, you understand."

WE LEFT THE MASTERS in a tense silence and gathered around my great-aunt's kitchen table. Agent Mayeux sat with us, although he was still so irate that he virtually levitated out of his chair.

"What in the devil's name made you three think that it was a good idea to follow us?"

Gertie shrugged. "It's a free country, isn't it?"

Kase groaned. "Did it not occur to you that you might be interfering?"

"Interfering in what, Mayeux?" Aunt Ida Belle's eyes flashed. "Why are you so het up about us joining you?"

"Joining us? Is that what you call it?" Kase pounded his fist on the table. "Try stalking."

"Don't flatter yourself, Agent." Fortune had been quiet up until this point. "Didn't I warn you at Francine's that we weren't going to be left out of whatever you're up to?"

I sat silently and listened as the verbal sparring continued. Fortune and Aunt Ida Belle were adamant that they were being lied to. Which they were. For his part, Agent Mayeux was insistent that they were being meddlesome. Which they were. For her part, Gertie simply cheered on whomever she felt was making a valid point. Clearly, she needed to get out more if this was her idea of entertainment. As for myself, I'd soon heard enough.

"Agent Mayeux, if I might just say something." I tried and failed to get his attention. "Kase, might I add my two cents," I tried again. No one at the table paid me any heed. I sat back in my chair and folded my hands. Fine. It had come to this. I cleared my throat in as ladylike a fashion as possible and spoke softly. "Honey?"

The frenzied four-way conversation immediately ceased as they turned in unison to face me. Finally.

"Honey?" Aunt Ida Belle asked, one eyebrow raised.

"I think she means Agent Hunky," Gertie said.

Fortune didn't try to hide her smirk.

Agent Mayeux turned to face me. "Yes, darlin'?"

Aunt Ida Belle smacked her palm into her forehead. "Oh, Lordy. If she's calling him 'honey' that means she's in deep."

"Enough of the bickering. Please. It's unproductive, not to mention unseemly." No one disagreed with me, so I continued. "Agent Mayeux and I need you three to kindly stop interfering in our plans."

Kase slung his arm across the back of my chair. He appeared pleased by my words, a look I knew wouldn't last for long. My next statement was bound to put the cat among the pigeons.

"We're trying to smoke out a drug dealer within the Masters family and—" but the rest of my sentence was drowned out by a simultaneous explosion of protests from Aunt Ida Belle, Gertie and Fortune.

And so, the feathers began to fly.

"How dare you put my niece in danger?"

"Lenora Masters deals drugs?"

"Why isn't the DEA looking into this?"

"What makes you think you can keep her safe?"

"No wonder she gets all those deliveries from New Orleans. Ha, and here I thought it was wrinkle cream she was having brought in by the truckload."

"Does Carter know you're snooping around?"

When the ladies gave no indication that they were near done lobbing questions, I held up my hands to call a ceasefire to the bombardment. "You're not going to get any answers if you won't let us speak."

Once order was established, I gestured to my great-aunt. "You may proceed after you indicate whether you have a comment or a question."

Aunt Ida Belle's brows knit into a ferocious scowl. "Oh, for the love of Pete—"

"Comment or question?" I reiterated.

"Agent Mayeux, do you seriously think I'm going to let you endanger Stephanie's life while you go poking around into a hornet's nest?"

"Technically a question, but I'll allow it." Frankly, I was more than a little curious to hear the answer myself. "Agent Mayeux?"

He didn't look any happier than my great-aunt. "I'm insulted that you think I'd use Stephanie for my own means. I'll protect her with my life. I give you my word."

Aunt Ida Belle made a noise that sounded very much like the air being let out of a car tire.

"My turn!" Gertie waved her hand in the air. "I've got a question."

"Go ahead."

"Does the FBI have any silver fox agents that you can call in as backup?"

"What are those?" Agent Mayeux looked to me for clarification, but I could only shrug. Perhaps they were an elite investigative team I'd never heard of.

"Silver fox, you know, like George Clooney. Pay Gertie no mind," my great-aunt interjected. "She's just man crazy."

Alrighty then. Best to move right along. "Fortune, do you have a question or comment?"

"Question." Surprisingly compliant, she waited for me to nod before she continued. "Agent Mayeux, does your superior have any idea what you're up to?" She cocked her head sideways. "Because something tells me that she or he would be more than a little interested."

"Now hold up, Fortune." I felt my cheeks flush. "That's hugely unfair of you to imply that Kase is doing anything inappropriate. Especially considering that your decision to drug him is what got him into hot water at work."

Kase gave my shoulder a gentle squeeze. "Thanks, darlin'."

Fortune shrugged. "You don't have to make it sound like I shot him with a horse tranquilizer. We're talking cookies and milk here. Besides, there's an element of danger in the work he does, as well as a chain of command and protocol that must be followed. He and I both know that."

Oh, yes, of course. She'd know all about the dangers he faced as a federal agent based on her imaginary time in the CIA. I resisted the temptation to call her out on her delusion. But I was going to have to talk to Aunt Ida Belle about this. Maybe she could convince Fortune to get professional help.

"Don't even go there," Kase growled. Clearly, he was still sensitive about the issue.

I clapped my hands together. "Let's focus on the matter at hand. Sinful has enough problems without becoming a hub for drug distribution."

"What kind of drugs?" Gertie asked.

"Geritol, for all we know. Does it matter?" I snapped. The words were barely out of my mouth before I regretted using such a snarky tone. "I'm sorry, Gertie. I have no right to be so unpleasant. Will you forgive me?"

Gertie's genuine smile reassured me that she didn't hold my momentary lapse in manners against me. "Of course I do, kiddo. For a second you sounded just like your aunt."

Fortune snickered. Aunt Ida Belle winked at me. I turned to look at Kase. His smile was sympathetic, for which I was grateful.

"It doesn't matter what they're running through here," he said. "Trafficking is an illegal activity, and narcotics of any kind are going to bring nothing but trouble to Sinful. We agree on that, obviously."

We nodded.

"All I'm proposing to do is use my administrative leave," he leveled a look at Fortune that I was glad wasn't directed toward me, "to see if I can get any sense of what's going on. I'm a professional agent and I know when to call in backup. Which I won't hesitate to do, if and when that time comes."

"What part is Stephanie playing in this?" Aunt Ida Belle had asked the question before, but this time her voice held less rancor, although her concern was still palpable. "She's an innocent, Mayeux. I'm not going to let her get hurt. Not on my watch."

Kase leaned forward, his voice low and intense. "Ida Belle, you have my word as a law enforcement officer of the United States government, as well as a man who cares deeply for your niece, that I won't allow her to come to any harm."

As their gazes locked, I willed myself not to appear as emotional as I felt. Hearing people expressing their concern for me wasn't something I was used to. It felt good. I took a deep, steadying breath. "It appears we're all on the same page, which is fortunate considering we're all in this together."

"We are?" Aunt Ida Belle and Agent Mayeux spoke as one.

"We most certainly are." I retrieved a pen and paper from the counter and sat back down amongst my co-conspirators. "Let's start with making a list."

I began to write. Task number one, find Gertie a suitable date for the wedding, preferably someone who owned a necktie. Task number two, find a cocktail dress for Fortune that was snug enough that she wouldn't be able to sneak a concealed weapon into the wedding reception. Task number three, I wrote, warming to my mission, get Aunt Ida Belle and Walter together for a dancing lesson so they could brush up on their Viennese waltz.

Fortune leaned over my shoulder, scanned my list, and gave a low whistle. "Uh, guys, I don't think we should let Stephanie lead the parade on this one."

I waved her away. "You don't get a vote, Fortune. Please sit down."

She returned to her seat, looking none too happy about my ascension to a leadership role. "You don't have the chops for this, Stephanie."

I set my pen down, folded my hands neatly in front of me, and met her gaze straight on. "I most certainly do. I'm the most qualified person here to infiltrate the Masters' wedding, and I can prove it."

She waved an impatient hand. "Go right ahead."

"Certainly. Now, imagine we're all seated at a round table for eight. There are four pieces of stemware at each place setting. Which is for white wine?" I paused, but just as I thought, no one did anything other than stare at me. I pressed on. "The appetizer course is over. Yet there are still three forks to your right. What are they for and in which order should they be used?"

Perhaps I should have let it go there but, let's face it, I was in my element. "When going through the reception line, whom would etiquette dictate be the first to greet us? The mother of the bride or the mother of the groom?" Again, I paused, as a courtesy. "Precisely my point. I'm in charge now."

Chapter Five

I LOVED THE IDEA OF acting as the ringleader in this latest rendition of the Sinful Circus. However, the day after proclaiming that I was in charge, I realized that I had no idea what we should do next. To clarify, I knew what steps to take to prepare the ladies for the actual wedding ceremony and reception. But when it came to the question of how to investigate which of the Masters family was involved in illegal activities, there I was stumped. Charm school hadn't prepared me for this type of task.

It was time to eat humble pie.

"Would you like a scoop of vanilla bean ice cream with this?" I asked as I slid a generously cut slice of Ally's Dutch Apple pie in front of the one person who could help me decide how to proceed. "Or would you prefer a cold glass of milk?"

Kase arched an eyebrow. "Seriously? You're offering me milk?"

"Oh, right, sorry." I pulled out a chair and sat across from him. We hadn't had a moment alone since our group meeting the day before. I'd called him to come over when Aunt Ida Belle went to meet Fortune and Gertie for lunch. "Surely you don't believe that I would drug you, do you?"

The few seconds he took to frame an answer could have offended a less confident woman.

"I don't know what to believe in this town."

"It was Fortune who drugged you, not me. Besides, I need your help, and that means I need you conscious."

"Fair enough." He picked up his fork and took another bite of pie. "This is unbelievably good," he said somewhere between the third and fourth bites. "You make it?"

I shook my head. "Ally did. The kitchen isn't the room where my particular talents shine." As soon as the words were out of my mouth, I realized how they sounded. Was I blushing again? I was. "I mean, I'm not—"

Kase held up his fork. "I got ya." He took a last bite of pie and pushed away his plate. "I just wondered, darlin', since we're dating and all, when can I expect a homemade meal?"

"I'll cook you the gourmet meal of your choice once you give me some advice on what to do next."

He leaned back in his chair and stretched his arms overhead. When he flexed his muscles, I swear the snake tattoo looked alive. "I thought you were taking the lead on this one."

"Smug doesn't suit you, Agent Mayeux."

"Did you ask your aunt and her friends for ideas?"

I bit my lip. If only humble pie went down as easily as Ally's did. "No. I'm honestly too embarrassed after the way I grandstanded about being in charge."

To my surprise, not to mention my immense relief, he didn't use my confession against me. Instead, he nodded. "I wouldn't exactly use the term grandstanded. You are the expert when it comes to etiquette, you weren't having one over on them there. Besides, even if you had a plan and laid it out for them, they'd still end up doing whatever they wanted."

"True." I blew out a long breath. "You have their number."

"Numbers that don't add up." His gaze was piercing, as if he expected me to understand what he wasn't saying as much as what he was. "I get the feeling that the unholy trinity aren't quite what they appear on the surface."

"Really? What makes you say that?"

"You haven't noticed anything different about them?" He leaned forward and rested his arms on the table. "Think, Stephanie."

I thought. And then it dawned on me what he meant. "Are you talking about Gertie's claims that Fortune was in the CIA?" I waved my hand. "I assure you that is simply the byproduct of Gertie's wild imagination. Fortune in the CIA? Please, nothing about that woman says 'federal agent.'"

"You're sure?"

I nodded emphatically. "Look, Kase, my great-aunt and Gertie are elderly ladies who have led very sheltered lives. Considering that they've always lived in Sinful, it's amazing that they've stayed as sane as they have. I think it's only natural that Gertie may sometimes exaggerate or that Aunt Ida Belle likes to act tough. But I assure you, they are what they seem."

"And Fortune?" he asked. "What's your take on her?"

I paused, not because I didn't have an opinion of her, but because I knew to tread carefully. It would be too easy to share that I thought she was a show-off who longed for attention. But there was nothing ladylike about discrediting someone behind her back. "I think that Fortune misses the beauty pageant circuit. Perhaps life as a librarian is a tad more boring than she expected it to be. To go from having so many people's eyes on you to being stuck in the book stacks can't be an easy transition."

He didn't respond but the way he watched me was unnerving.

"So you can see my dilemma about what to do with the three of them while we investigate. I mean, while you investigate and I assist."

He drummed his fingers on the table while he considered my words. "We need to throw them off track somehow. The spotlight should be on your Miss Prim and Proper persona—"

"It's not a persona," I cut him off. "It's who I am."

"All the time?"

I nodded.

"No periods of wild abandonment in your life?"

I sat up straight and squared my shoulders. "Most certainly not."

"You're not ever driven by passion? Don't you ever want to let your hair down and do something just because it feels good?"

I swallowed. His words, perhaps innocent enough on the surface, still managed to fuel a surge of warmth that shot through me. "No," I finally managed to say.

"If you say so, darlin.'"

"What were you saying about the spotlight?" I attempted to nudge him back toward the safer subject of drug dealers.

"Making sure the focus is on Miss Prim and Proper is the best way to distract the Masters family. All I want to do is lurk around and see what I can pick up on, that's it. But to do that, we need to get you in over there and keep your friends out."

"But keeping them out, as you say, is going to be virtually impossible now that they know what we're up to." I experienced a stab of contriteness. "Which is all my fault for blurting out your plans."

"Don't blame yourself," he said. "They'd have hounded us until they pieced it together anyway, so maybe it's for the best they know."

"Are they going to ruin your chances of finding something out?"

"Not if we keep them on a short leash."

"Oh, well, if that's all." I couldn't help but smile at the very tall order. "We're going to have to keep our wits about us."

Agent Mayeux nodded. "You're not kidding." He gestured to the empty dessert plate. "How about another slice of that pie?"

"Certainly." I stood and picked up the plate. "Ice cream this time?"

"A glass of milk, I think." He waited until I had taken a glass from the cupboard before he spoke again. "Stephanie, darlin?"

I glanced over my shoulder. "Yes?"

"I take my coffee black and my milk without sedatives."

"NO FISHNET STOCKINGS. I mean it Gertie." I settled my hands on my hips, ready to do battle over this edict if it came to that. I wasn't going to budge. "I'll wrestle them off of you myself if I have to."

Gertie's expression was petulant. "Why does Fortune get to wear black leather?"

Because she's thirty plus years younger than you and can pull it off was my first thought. I left this unsaid. Instead, I voiced my second thought, "Because it supports her mission."

Aunt Ida Belle rolled her eyes. "Since when is getting hit on by a twenty-something-year old punk with a drug habit considered a mission?"

I drew myself up to my full height. Kase had advised me to appear unwavering in my command of the situation, and I was doing my best to follow his instructions. But these ladies weren't making it easy. I tapped my watch. "We need to leave for the bridal shower in less than ten minutes. Agent Mayeux should be here with the car soon, so let's finish getting ready. Gertie, strip those stockings off. Now."

While she clearly wasn't happy about following my directions, she did as I bid. To show my appreciation, I ignored her mumbled comment about uppity Yankee whippersnappers. I gave my great-aunt a cursory going over. She passed muster. She'd refused to wear a skirt but had at least ditched her blue jeans for a pair of dark slacks. A white blouse completed her look. Simple but acceptable. Fortune, who'd been assigned to cozy up to Shawn, wore a short black leather skirt paired with a simple scoop-necked black t-shirt. It wasn't a look that screamed 'bridal shower', but hopefully it would be enough to loosen Shawn's tongue.

"Well, ladies," I said, stretching that last word to within the very limits of its definition, "it's show time. You have your instructions. Please stick to my plan. This is a reconnaissance mission only." I held up three fingers and ticked them off as I spoke. "Therefore, no one should put anyone in a headlock, no one should brandish a weapon, and, above all else, no one should do anything that might get them disinvited from the wedding. Am I clear?"

After I'd secured a reluctant agreement from each of them, I ushered them downstairs. Adrenaline coursed through my body. I'd managed to whip together an impromptu bridal shower within the space of seventy-two hours. On top of that, I'd secured invitations for Gertie, Fortune and Ida Belle to the wedding on Saturday. Truly, we lived in a time of miracles.

"Please don't forget your gifts." I handed each of them a present as they headed for the front door. I'd personally selected gifts for the bride and had wrapped them in elegant black and silver paper with a light pink bow made of French ribbon.

True to his promise, Agent Mayeux had somehow procured a town car spacious enough for all of us. I thanked him as I slipped into the front seat. His only response was to wink as he shut my door.

The drive to the Masters house passed surprisingly quickly and quietly. I felt a sudden surge of confidence that everything would go along today just as we'd planned. I would keep an eye on the bride-to-be, her mother, and her step-mother. Gertie was supposed to circulate among the guests and see if she could pick up any gossip that might be a clue that would help Kase. "Listen, don't talk," I'd advised her several times, but I suspected that advice fell on deaf ears. My great-aunt was meant to keep an eye on Lenora. "An eye," I'd reminded her, "not a hand." Fortune, for her part, was tasked with seeing what she could find out from Cassandra's brother.

If all went according to plan, this would allow Agent Mayeux to loiter around, as he put it. When I'd pressed him for details he'd simply said, "The less you know, darlin', the better." Fine. It wasn't like I didn't have my own part to play in all of this. Lenora had readily agreed to host the shower at her home, and in return I had promised her to take on the role of hostess so that she could relax and enjoy the day.

I looked over my shoulder. "Remember that it's as simple as mix, mingle, smile, and listen."

Kase shot me a skeptical look. Oh, right. This was Sinful. The town where nothing was ever as simple as one, two, three. Silly me.

Chapter Six

THE FIRST THIRTY MINUTES of the bridal shower went precisely according to plan. As the guests who'd come in from New Orleans mingled with the ladies from Sinful, I sipped champagne from a crystal flute and silently congratulated myself on accomplishing what had seemed impossible at the outset. Thanks to Kase's money, and my excellent taste, we'd managed to create an elegant affair.

"Oh, Stephanie, this has just been the loveliest surprise." The guest of honor stood at my side, her smile wide and her eyes bright. "I didn't think I was going to even have a shower, least of all one this elegant."

"That surprises me, Cassandra. Surely your mother or grandmother had planned one for you?"

She shook her head. "My mother and step-mother were arguing about the idea so much that my dad put a stop to it by saying I didn't need a shower. And Grandmother is a recluse at heart. She'd never have opened her home to a bunch of people she didn't know, even if they were friends of mine."

"But she's hosting your wedding," I objected. "Here at her home for several hundred people. Hardly the act of a hermit."

Cassandra shrugged. "Weird, I know. No one was more surprised than I was when she offered to have the wedding and reception here, trust me. But she's been an angel about it.

Everything I've wanted, she agreed to immediately. Well, except for one thing."

I made every effort to appear nonchalant, although I felt anything but. "Oh, really? What was that?" I took a sip of champagne. With any luck, she'd give me an interesting tidbit of information, however small, that I could take back to Kase.

"Grandmother was insistent that she pick the date and the time for the ceremony."

A follow-up question was halfway formed on my lips when one of Cassandra's sorority sisters joined us. After a brief chat, I excused myself so that I could go in search of Agent Mayeux.

It took me a few moments, but I found him wandering the grounds. He looked surprised to see me.

"Shouldn't you be in there keeping an eye on things up at the house?" he asked.

"I'm happy to report that everything is under control. Fortune, Gertie, and my great-aunt are absolute role models of proper behavior." I said this with a feeling akin to pride. Agent Mayeux took off his sunglasses and stared down at me. "And doesn't that fact have you just a little worried?"

"No, of course not." I thought a moment. "Should it?"

"Fortune's sipping tea from a china cup, Ida Belle is sitting quietly making small talk with a group of ladies, and, last I saw, Gertie has managed to keep her clothes on." He lifted an eyebrow. "Personally, I'd be worried."

"Yes, I see your point." I bit my lip, unsure of what to do about it, though. "Well, I did implore them to behave themselves. Did it ever occur to you that they might be enjoying acting like ladies?"

"Acting's the right word for it." Kase gave a half-laugh. "Trust me, darlin', if you go up there and let them off their leashes, they'll be grateful." He gave a quick look around to ensure that we were alone. "Besides, I've done everything out here that I can. I want to poke around the second story. Chaos would be a helpful distraction. I need twenty minutes or less."

"Chaos," I repeated. "I think that can be arranged." Who was I kidding? Chaos was second nature to these women.

Kase took a step toward me, closing the distance between us. He reached out and laid his hands on my shoulders. "Stephanie, the whole reason we came up with the idea of a shower was to have another excuse to be here on the premises. Never mind all the crazy adults who live in this town. Sinful is full of young kids. Drugs have no business passing through here."

I nodded. "You're right. I've just enjoyed the relative calm so far."

"Yes, but the fact that everything is going so smoothly is reason enough for people to get suspicious. This is Sinful, after all." His eyes met mine.

I was having the utmost difficulty looking away even though I knew I should go back. I took a deep breath. "I'd better go."

Kase leaned in and brushed a kiss across my forehead. "Keep an eye on the front staircase and don't let anyone go up. Can you do that?"

I nodded. The way my heart was beating in my chest, I'd pretty much have agreed to anything he asked of me. As I made my way up to the house, I forced myself to not look back. What little dignity I still possessed, I needed to keep intact.

INCITING THE LADIES into riotous action took virtually no effort on my part. First, I made eye contact with Fortune, who appeared to instinctively understand that it was time to swing into action. She excused herself from the group she was sitting with and headed toward the foyer. A quick glance over my shoulder assured me that Shawn, who had been lurking in the room next door, was on her tail. I heard the front door close behind them. I shook my head. That poor, cocky kid.

Despite stopping along the way to exchange pleasantries with a few guests, I made it across the room within a matter of minutes. I drew my great-aunt aside first. "Aunt Ida Belle, I need your help," I said in a hushed tone. "Kase needs a few moments upstairs, so he asked that we create a distraction." The flash of excitement in her eyes at the word distraction gave me pause. I laid my hand on her arm. "A small distraction, mind you. Nothing major."

She patted my hand before removing it from her person. "Consider me the Queen of Distraction." She turned so her back was to the room and reached into her cleavage. My eyes widened when I saw what she pulled out.

"Oh, no, Aunt Ida Belle." My stomach rolled over. "Put that back. Better yet, give it to me." I held out my hand.

Aunt Ida Belle shook her head. "Sorry, Stephanie. You can't have it both ways. You want a distraction but you also want me to sit around with these old biddies and act like we're at a hemorrhoid convention? What kind of plan is that?"

To save my life, I couldn't think of a response, especially not with that visual.

"Trust me, kiddo. Let me do my thing while you go watch out for your boyfriend." Before I could grab hold of her arm, she stepped out of my reach. I cringed as she clapped her hands together. "Quiet everyone, please. It's time for a game." She sounded all-together too pleased with herself. "We all love a good bridal shower game, don't we, gals?"

I hightailed it over to Gertie as the guests cheered. But before I could say anything, Aunt Ida Belle lifted the offending object over her head and swung it around. "Anyone ever play 'Pin the Tail on the Bitch?'"

I sucked in a lungful of air and spluttered it right back out again. "Gertie, help," I hissed. I pointed to the furry tail that Aunt Ida Belle was brandishing. "You have to do something."

"Damn straight." With a reassuring nod in my direction, she plunged into the crowd that was forming around my great-aunt. "Hold on, Ida Belle," she shouted, waving her arms over her head. "Don't do anything until I can take bets on how long it takes you to pin the biggest ass in the room."

Horror such as I'd never experienced washed over me. This was worse than the time that I was kidnapped by a Russian mob boss. Worse than the time I watched Aunt Ida Belle confess to a murder she didn't commit. Worse than the time I thought I'd lost my precious cat, Priscilla, to an alligator. Worse than the time—I gasped. Kase. I was supposed to be keeping an eye on the stairs. I rushed to the doorway and planted myself squarely in the center of it. Not that I needed have worried about blocking a mass exodus. All eyes were on the spectacle that was my nearest and dearest relative.

I cringed when I heard the crash of dishes hitting the floor. I bit my lip through the chants of "Pin her, pin her". I squeezed my eyes shut when someone cried, "Not the cake!" and then the choir-like gasp that followed. But through the sounds of my carefully planned bridal shower being destroyed, I didn't abandon my post.

An eternity passed before I caught sight of Kase coming down the stairs toward me. "It's about time. I need you to go in there and break up whatever's going on."

Kase jogged down the last few steps to stand by my side. "No one's called for an ambulance, have they? That's a good sign."

"Not funny." It annoyed me that he didn't appear the least bit fazed by the bedlam around us. "You do realize that after this debacle, none of us will be welcome at the wedding."

He reached out and chucked my chin. "Somehow I trust you'll smooth things over."

I pointed in the direction of the party. "There's no recovering from this."

And then, like a cannonball, Fortune shot out from the back of the house, pausing only to say, "Heads up, Donny Masters is here and he's pissed." She ran straight into the ruckus that was occurring in the living room.

"Damn." Kase made a move toward the front door, but when it was pushed open from the other side, he swung back around to face me. "Work with me here."

"What? How?"

He pulled me into his arms and held me tightly against his chest. "I don't want Masters to see my face." He turned us so that my back was up against the wall, and then he lowered his lips to mine in what was a most convincing kiss.

The front door shook as a man with dark hair and an even darker scowl slammed it shut. "What the hell is going on here?" He growled. "And who the hell are you two?"

Chapter Seven

"THAT WENT WELL."

"You know, Gertie, it's a little hard for me to take you seriously when you have fragments of cake and icing all over your person." I blew out a long breath as I dropped into one of Gertie's kitchen chairs. I was so far beyond exhausted that it was pathetic. Despite their advanced ages, I couldn't keep up with either Aunt Ida Belle or Gertie, physically or mentally. "You're a frightful mess."

Gertie grinned. "Yeah, but you should have seen the other gals."

I closed my eyes. Oh, I'd seen them all right. A vision of shower guests covered in bits of beautifully decorated cake, with their hair rumpled and their dresses askew, flashed through my mind in high definition technicolor. My picture-perfect shower had morphed into an out-and-out rumble.

Aunt Ida Belle snapped her fingers in front of my face. My eyes flew open. She didn't look half as giddy as Gertie did, but neither did she look tired. Far from it.

"Cold beer?" She held a bottle out to me but I shook my head. She pulled out a chair and sat beside me. "Suit yourself." She flipped the bottle cap off with a fork and took a long sip. When she was done, she set the half-empty bottle on the table and met my gaze. "Seems we scared your boyfriend away."

I managed not to blurt out that Kase wasn't my boyfriend, even though the disclaimer automatically sprang to my lips. "He said he was going to stop somewhere for a quick beer. He'll be back to pick me up when he's done."

"Unless he's hightailing it back to New Orleans about now," Gertie suggested. "To file a report with the FBI about what happened at the Masters'."

"About what happened at the Masters?" Fortune repeated, sounding every bit as incredulous as I felt. "Which part would he report? The part where Ida Belle pinned the tail on the ass, or the part where said ass turned into the hostess with a bionic arm who managed to slug three different women in an attempt to inflict damage on Ida Belle, her sworn mortal enemy?"

"What exactly happened between you two?" curiosity compelled me to ask. "Didn't Lenora say it had to do with Walter?"

Aunt Ida Belle stared down at her beer bottle for a long moment. "Sort of."

Fortune and I exchanged a knowing glance. When Aunt Ida Belle was being elusive, it meant there was a story there. We waited, but she didn't elaborate.

"I'll tell them," Gertie offered.

"No." Aunt Ida Belle set her drink on the table with a decided thud. "You'll just screw it up with some imaginary romantic mumbo jumbo."

I'd never seen my great-aunt look more uncomfortable. "Have you always been in love with Walter?" I asked.

Her frown was ferocious. "Who said I was in love with him?"

"There's nothing wrong with being in love, Ida Belle," Fortune said, her voice uncharacteristically gentle. "No one here would judge you if you admitted you loved Walter."

"The only idiot who's gone around mooning over Walter LeBlanc is Lenora Masters. She's never even tried to hide it." Aunt

Ida Belle's disgust was clear. "She embarrassed him and damn near humiliated herself in the process of trying to lure him into marriage."

"Yet he managed to avoid her trap," I said. "Because he was in love with you?"

"It's all damn fool nonsense." Ida Belle pushed away from the table and got to her feet without looking any one of us in the eye. "You want details? Fine. Lenora chased Walter. Walter ran. The cow blamed me. End of story." She picked up her empty beer bottle. "Anyone else want another?"

When we demurred, she stomped into the kitchen. "And don't talk about me behind my back. Gertie doesn't know squat and you two don't need to be knee deep in my personal business."

Fortune leaned in toward me from across the table. "Let's let this go for now. I'll work on getting the story out of Walter and you work on Gertie."

I nodded my agreement, although I would have much rather been tasked with speaking to Walter. At least he didn't speak in concentric circles the way Gertie did.

Fortune leaned back in her chair as my great-aunt rejoined us. "So, that Donny Masters is a nasty piece of work, isn't he?"

To this, I could agree whole-heartedly. He'd been in a foul temper when he'd slammed into his step-mother's house. Then he'd caught sight of Kase and me kissing, or pretending to kiss, although it certainly had felt real to me... I shook my head. *Focus, Stephanie.* The sight of us together had only served to further anger Lenora's step-son. Donny had demanded to know who we were but to his credit, Kase didn't turn around and go off on when Donny called him a Neanderthal. That amount of self-restraint either spoke well of Kase's FBI training or of his inner strength and ability to control himself. I, however, hadn't been able to hold my tongue, and I gave Donny Masters more than an earful about the respectful way to enter a home and greet his step-mother's guests. Finally, Donny had grown disgusted and ordered us to leave.

"He's definitely a piece of work," Aunt Ida Belle said. "But the whole family is whacked in the head if you want my opinion."

"Word," Gertie agreed.

"What I can't figure out is why Kase was so anxious for Donny to not see his face." I slipped off my heels and rubbed my tired feet. "Unless they've met before?"

Fortune shook her head. "I doubt it's that. But think about it, Stephanie, if Donny is the mastermind behind the drug running, he'd be wary of anyone he finds hanging around his turf, right?"

I nodded as if this had occurred to me already. It hadn't.

"Between your boyfriend's size, distinctive tattoo, and the way he carries himself, it would be easy for Donny to ask around about him."

"The man's a hunky hulk." Gertie rubbed her hands together. "Hubba hubba."

Fortune rolled her eyes. "As opposed to these two," she motioned to Aunt Ida Belle and Gertie with her head. "Two old women can fly under the radar because, well, they're two old women."

"Bite me," Aunt Ida Belle growled.

"All I'm saying is that a man like Donny Masters is likely to underestimate two intelligent women like you simply because of your age and gender."

I nodded. I could see that. In the short amount of time I spoke with him I found him to be imperious, condescending, demanding, and ill-mannered. "So, you think he's the mastermind?"

Fortune shrugged. "He could be. Or he could just be a total jerk-off, hard to tell."

"What about his son?"

"The kid uses." Something on my face must have indicated I wasn't following her. "Drugs," she clarified. "He's got a drug problem. Not to mention a serious attitude problem. The little punk wouldn't take no for an answer. He was absolutely determined to get his hand up my skirt. I almost had to break his wrist."

I flinched at her casual tone. These women weren't playing. Which made it all the more important that we get to the bottom of this before someone got hurt. "What about Donny's ex-wife? Did any of you get a chance to talk to Kitty?"

"I thought that you were going to do that."

"I tried, Aunt Ida Belle. But Kitty's terrified of her own shadow. She'd barely make eye contact, let alone small talk. I think we can safely cross her off our list."

The other women exchanged one of their "Stephanie is clueless" looks.

"You can't take everyone at face value, kid." Aunt Ida Belle clapped a hand on my shoulder. "Either the woman is a mouse or she's a lion who wants you to think she's a mouse."

"What about Carmen, then?" Was I supposed to think she was weak or meek because it was the opposite of the strong, tough image she projected?

"She's interesting," Fortune said. "She comes across as a real ball-buster—"

I flinched at her choice of words.

"—but she also strikes me as intelligent. I wouldn't underestimate her."

Aunt Ida Belle nodded. "She strikes me as a bit of a caricature with that accent. Hard to believe it's real."

"Her boobs sure aren't," Gertie chuckled. "What about the daughter?"

"Surely you don't suspect Cassandra?" Astonished, I looked between them. "But she's the bride."

"Which means what exactly? She's incapable of committing a crime because she's making wedding plans?"

I bristled at Fortune's tone. "What bride would jeopardize her wedding with illegal activities?"

"One who stood to make high six figures in a single night."

I shrugged and looked away. Where was Kase? I found that I was craving his company. He was the most normal person in Sinful, and right about now normal sounded heavenly. "So basically, even after all of the nonsense we endured today, not to mention all the money and time we spent making plans, we're no closer to discovering anything than we were before the shower?" What a depressing thought.

"Depends on what your boyfriend might have uncovered." Fortune glanced at her watch. "Wonder what's keeping him? I'm surprised he's not here taking us to task for how things went down."

"Well, the good news is that we're all still invited to the wedding." Gertie looked inordinately proud of that fact. "Lenora didn't revoke our invitations."

"Yet." I got to my feet. "Shall I make sandwiches for everyone?"

They readily agreed. I didn't doubt they were hungry, seeing as how they'd been too busy flinging cake to actually eat any. As for myself, I was happy to have a quiet moment alone to think. The other ladies didn't seem especially discouraged, but I felt like we'd wasted an entire day, not to mention that we'd made an absolute spectacle out of ourselves. Poor Cassandra.

We ate in relative silence. I refused their offers to help me wash up because I knew there was a basketball game on TV that they wanted to watch. As kind as the ladies had been to me, and there was no denying they'd welcomed me when I'd needed a place to hide, I didn't fit in here. I belonged back in Boston. As soon as Kase finished up with his investigation and didn't need me to pretend to be his girlfriend, it would be time for Priscilla and me to head back to Massachusetts. I put away the last glass and wiped my hands on a dish towel, feeling strangely disquieted by how unsettling the thought of leaving was, even though I thought that was what I wanted.

The doorbell sounded as I re-entered the living room. "I'll get it." Their eyes were glued to the ballgame, so no one put up an argument. I was relieved to know that Kase was back. He felt like an ally, if only because we were both Sinful outsiders.

Except that when I opened the front door, it wasn't Agent Mayeux who stood on Gertie's doorstep. It was Carter.

"Where's Kase?" he asked without preamble.

"In town having a beer. Why?"

"Where exactly? Did he say?"

His pensive expression unnerved me. I touched my strand of pearls. "Carter, what's wrong?"

"There's been a report of an attempted murder."

Chapter Eight

ATTEMPTED MURDER? MY knees sagged and I grabbed on to the door for support. I must have cried out because within seconds Aunt Ida Belle was right behind me. She put a comforting arm around my shoulders.

"What's going on, Carter?" she demanded. "You'd better have a good excuse for upsetting my niece."

"Someone tried to kill Donny Masters tonight."

"That's as good a reason as any, I suppose." She gently drew me back inside and motioned for Carter to come through. "Come in and tell us what you know."

"Why are you so anxious to locate Kase?" I asked, as I dropped onto the couch. "Is he in danger?"

By this time, Gertie had turned off the television. Fortune crossed to stand beside Carter, her hand on the small of his back.

"Who called it in?" Fortune asked.

"His wife. Ex-wife actually." He slipped an arm around her waist. "Kitty Masters. She's the one who found him. To say she was freaked out would be the understatement of the century."

"Was he shot?" Gertie asked. "Or did someone try to feed him to a gator?"

Carter nodded. "Shot at, or so he claims."

"What do you mean by that?" Aunt Ida Belle demanded. "Was he shot at or wasn't he?"

Carter looked tired. He rubbed his eyes. "That's what he claims. Deputy Breaux is over there now digging a bullet out of the boat house."

"Why are you asking where Kase is? Do you have reason to believe he's in danger?" And then, as the words left my lips, another thought occurred to me. Did Carter suspect that Kase had somehow been involved in the shooting? I clenched my hands.

"I don't think he's in danger," Carter answered. But I grew increasingly uncomfortable when he didn't say more.

"Well, what do you want to talk to him about then?" Gertie demanded.

Bless her, the woman tap-danced where angels didn't dare tip-toe.

Carter didn't try to hide his exasperation. "That's between Mayeux and me," he all but snapped. "I swear the fact there's four of you now is keeping me up nights."

Under other circumstances I would have been quite flattered to have been counted in as one of the "gang", but I still wasn't completely satisfied as to why Carter felt a pressing need to speak with Kase. Therefore, I was neither going to be flattered nor share any information.

"We'll, he's not here." I stood. "Now, if you'll excuse me, I'm going to head back to my great-aunt's house and get some sleep."

My pronouncement effectively broke up our little meeting. Carter returned to the Masters, Gertie and Fortune decided to heat up a casserole, and Aunt Ida Belle wanted to stay and join them. I insisted that I was going to walk home.

The evening air, while not exactly cool, was at least fresh, and it felt good on my face as I headed back to Aunt Ida Belle's house. I was about half way home when my skin prickled as an uneasy sensation came over me. I glanced over my shoulder, but I didn't see anything besides the usual shadows cast by streetlights. Still, I hastened my steps.

I'd covered another block and just passed a wide oak tree when a dark shadow loomed in front of me. I barely had time to gasp before the shadow wrapped a thick arm around me. A hand covered my mouth as I was lifted off the ground.

"Don't scream," the voice intoned to ward off what was the most natural of reactions under these circumstances. "For cryin' out loud, Stephanie, it's me."

Kase? My relief quickly gave way to anger and I struggled harder, which didn't help me break free of his hold. I bit one of the fingers he had clamped over my mouth. Kase yelped and loosened his hold just enough that I managed to get my two feet planted on solid ground. I whirled around and stared up at him. "Kase Mayeux, what is the matter with you?" My voice shook with anger. "How dare you sneak up and grab me like that?"

He opened his mouth to respond, whether to apologize or justify his behavior, I didn't give him an opportunity to say. I was still flooded with adrenaline. "To grab an unsuspecting lady, in the dark, is the very height of ill manners." What else could I say? That covered it. Rather than wait for a response, I set out in the direction of my great-aunt's house.

It took no effort on his part to catch up with me. He had to slow his steps so that he didn't outpace me. Whatever. I wasn't the least bit sympathetic. My heart was still hammering in my chest.

"I'm sorry, Stephanie, forgive me," he said. "But I wanted to catch you."

I rolled my eyes even though he couldn't see it in the dark. "I believe that you could have done that with a loud whisper, a telephone call, or a text." I picked up my pace.

"You're right. I'm sorry. But I wanted to—"

"Catch me, so you said."

He stopped walking and laid a hand on my arm. "Hear me out. Please."

I stopped. What was I going to do? It wasn't like I could out-run him. And, truthfully, a little part of me was curious about the cloak and dagger routine. Was something going on? Or had the good agent simply been in town long enough to start showing signs of the 'Sinful crazies'?

"Talk fast."

"How would you feel about going on a stake-out tonight?"

This was the last thing I'd expected to hear. "A stake-out?"

He nodded. "There's been some action over at the Masters' mansion. I want to go over there and see if anything else is going to happen tonight."

"But surely Carter's deputies will be there?"

Kase shook his head. "Nope, LeBlanc doesn't have the manpower. Come with me."

I cocked my head and considered his request. I had to admit the idea intrigued me. I'd been to tea parties, polo matches, garden weddings, and classical concerts in the park on lovely summer evenings, but never on a stake-out. "Why are you so anxious for me to accompany you?"

"Having you along provides me with cover." He must have sensed that I didn't fully understand. "If someone comes across the two of us sitting in my truck out in the middle of nowhere, they'll assume we're up to, well, you know."

"Quite." It made sense. In a Sinful sort of way. And then a thought occurred to me. "But why are you sneaking around like this? Why not just call me? I've already agreed to play my part as your girlfriend this week."

"Because I want you. Not your family and friends. I've had enough crazy for today."

"You'll get no argument from me on that." I thought a moment. "Okay. I need to go back to Aunt Ida Belle's house so that I can feed Priscilla. I'll change and leave a note that we've gone to Mudbug."

"You think they'll buy that?"

I shrugged. "It's worth a try to send them in the wrong direction in case they decide to follow us."

We made short work of checking on the world's most precious Persian. I swiftly changed into a pair of white denim capris. Was white a smart color choice for a stakeout? I supposed so. It wasn't like we were going on a trek, at least I hoped not. I paired the capris with a red and white gingham top with puffed sleeves that I'd picked up in New Orleans on Gertie's urging. Although what possessed me to take fashion advice from her, I can't explain. But Kase's appreciative expression when I rushed downstairs was gratifying. I left a note that Kase and I were going to Mudbug and I might be home late.

We didn't talk as Kase drove toward the Masters' property. Once there, he guided the truck off-road, drove through a field behind their property line, slipped the truck into park, and cut the engine.

"The lake is just over there," he said, pointing into the darkness.

"I'll take your word for that." It was too dark for me to see anything. I will say that the stars shone brilliantly. However, I was deeply grateful that we were in a locked vehicle and not traipsing around outside. Between the alligators and a shooter that might be lurking nearby, the cramped cab of a truck suited me just fine, thank you very much.

I'd had more than enough fun for one day.

"STEPHANIE, WAKE UP."

Although the words were whispered, they somehow broke through my slumber. I sat up. I was still in Kase's truck, asleep on my first stake-out. Hardly impressive. I looked over at him. He looked like it was the middle of the morning after a good night's sleep. "Sorry, I fell asleep."

His only answer was a nod. His eyes were focused on something outside. I rubbed my eyes and tried to focus but the only thing I took in was an all-encompassing darkness.

"I'll be right back, darlin'." He already had one hand on the door handle. "Stay put."

I held my breath for several long seconds after Kase disappeared into the darkness. *Breathe, Stephanie, breathe.* Horrific visions of Kase being attacked by an alligator danced in my mind's eye. I didn't even want to think what might happen if he interrupted someone making a drop. My only source of comfort was that the passenger window was open a tiny bit and I didn't hear tortured screams. I counted to one hundred at least twelve times before Kase returned to the truck. Without a word, he turned the engine over and we started back the way we'd come. He didn't turn the lights on until we were on the road.

"False alarm?" I asked, wondering what had put the frown on his face.

"We'll let Carter and the divers he's going to have to call in decide that." He looked over at me and favored me with a half-smile. "You okay, darlin'?"

Agent Kase Mayeux was sexier than he had the right to be, but if he didn't already know that he wasn't about to learn it from me. I schooled my features so that I looked like I was at a board meeting. "Certainly. Just another stake-out." I appreciated his being kind enough not to mention that I'd napped through more than half of it. "What's this about divers?"

"I'd bet ninety-nine cents to a dollar that I just witnessed the gun that was used to take a potshot at Donny Masters being thrown into their lake."

"Really?" I shifted in my seat. "What makes you so sure it was a gun?"

"What else do you think someone at a crime scene is going to want to sneak out and dispose of in the middle of the night?"

"Right, I see your point." I thought a moment. "I don't suppose you saw who it was that was doing the throwing?"

Kase nodded. "I most certainly did."

"And are you going to tell me who it was?"

"None other than the mother of the bride-to-be, Kitty Masters."

Chapter Nine

"JUST WHAT WERE YOU two young'uns doing in Mudbug this late?" Aunt Ida Belle appeared none too pleased as she looked between Kase and me. We stood on her front porch as if we were two shamefaced teenagers rather than the professional, independent adults we actually were.

"We know what they were doing," Gertie piped up from the porch swing, her voice decidedly merry for so late in the evening. "We just don't know why they had to go all the way to Mudbug to do it."

Kase slipped his arm around my waist and leaned down to whisper in my ear, "Aren't senior citizens supposed to be early to bed and early to rise?"

"We're also supposed to be hard of hearing, but I just heard every impudent word you said." Aunt Ida Belle fixed a stern glance on Kase.

"I left a note," I said in our defense. "It wasn't our intention to cause you any distress."

Fortune settled next to Gertie on the porch swing. "I don't think your aunt's upset with you, Stephanie. I think she's actually concerned that she might have missed out on something related to the attempted shooting. Any truth to that, Ida Belle?"

"Oh, hell's bells." My great-aunt threw up her hands. "Guilty as charged. I hate getting left behind."

"You didn't miss much, although we did learn one thing that was interesting." I motioned toward the house. "Shall we go inside?"

"You go ahead, ladies. I'm going to track down LeBlanc." Agent Mayeux leaned down and deposited a gentle kiss on top of my head. "Try not to miss me too much, darlin'." He waved as he walked toward his truck but then stopped and looked back. "I highly recommend you ladies stay safely inside until morning."

I stifled a groan. Those words were tantamount to waving a red flag in front of this crowd. I shepherded them inside and soon we were back at the kitchen table, also known as Shenanigans Command Central.

"So, what'd you find out?" my great-aunt asked.

"Agent Mayeux—"

Gertie held up her hand. "Stephanie, if you and Agent Sex Pot are really dating, shouldn't you call him by his first name?"

"Oh, right. We drove out to do some surveillance behind the lake at the back of the Masters' property—"

This time it was my great-aunt who interrupted me. "Then what was that cockamamie story about going to Mudbug?"

I suddenly felt exhausted. Why weren't these two women, both decades older than I, showing signs of fatigue? "Kase contended that if you knew where we were, and what we were doing, you'd have joined us. I agreed with him. Was he wrong?" My great-aunt's silence was all the admission that I was likely to get. I pressed on. "I lost track of how long we'd been waiting." Why mention that I'd dozed off? It wouldn't earn me points with this group. "But eventually Kase caught sight of someone and followed them."

"Was it Donny Masters?" Fortune asked.

I shook my head.

"The Colombian bombshell?" Gertie asked.

Again, I shook my head. "Guess again."

"Like hell I will," Aunt Ida Belle grumbled. "Put us out of our misery."

"It was Kitty." I could see their surprise. "Kase saw her pitch something, a gun he thinks, into the lake. He's gone to tell Carter what he suspects about the drugs."

"So he said." Aunt Ida Belle scratched her head, her brows knit into a frown. "Who knew mousy little Kitty had it in her to destroy evidence?"

"You never really know about people." Fortune blew out a long breath. "Now we just need to figure out why she threw the gun in the lake."

What? Fortune was having trouble understanding Kitty's actions? And we were supposed to believe that she was an undercover operative? Ha. CIA agent my left foot. "To get rid of it, obviously," I said.

Their expressions were pitying. "Yes, Stephanie, we've worked out that much," my great-aunt said. "But why? Was it because she used it to take a shot at her ex-husband? Or did she know who shot him and wanted to stop them from trying again?"

"If it were Shawn or Cassandra, it's only natural she'd want to shield her children." Gertie absentmindedly stroked Priscilla, who was curled up on a chair of her own. "I doubt she'd want to protect Charo. There can't be any love lost between those two."

I pressed my fingertips to my temples. We weren't getting anywhere, and the more we talked about it, the less sense it all made. "I feel bad that we weren't able to help Kase discover anything concrete. Cassandra's wedding was the only reason we had for being anywhere near the Masters. But now we don't have a single excuse to be in their world."

Gertie met my eye. "It ain't over until it's over, kiddo."

"But it is," I protested. "Now that the wedding's been called off—"

"Where'd you hear that?" my great-aunt demanded.

My eyebrows rose. "You can't seriously believe that there's going to be a wedding after someone tried to kill the bride's father?"

"Sure I can," she shot back. "Almost murdered and murdered are two very different things."

"Gotta agree," Gertie chimed in. "If they aren't throwing a funeral by the day after tomorrow, they'll be throwing a wedding."

Throwing a funeral? Was that how it was done here in Sinful? I shuddered to think. Today's bridal shower had been bad enough. I stood. "It's been an incredibly long day. Anyone else think it's time to call it a night?"

Everyone agreed. We made it as far as the front hall when the doorbell rang. We exchanged puzzled looks. Aunt Ida Belle looked out the peep hole. "Mercy me," she whispered. "It's the blushing bride."

Cassandra? What was she doing here this late?

We found out soon enough. Within minutes we were back at the kitchen table. Yet another plate of Ally's cookies sat in the middle of the table. I poured several glasses of milk. Gertie had suggested a round of cough syrup shots, but I vetoed that idea. I still had my standards. Perhaps Cassandra had come to collect apologies from each of us for ruining her bridal shower. Fair enough. I'd start.

"I can't apologize enough for what happened today." I set a glass of milk in front of her and sat beside her. "You deserved so much better than that. I'm sorry."

She reached out and squeezed my hand. "I don't blame you." She cast a polluted look at my great-aunt first, then at Gertie, and lastly at Fortune. "We all know who's to blame and it certainly isn't you, Stephanie."

I was torn. Family loyalty dictated that I rush to Aunt Ida Belle's defense. I looked across the table at her. She was a gruff woman at times, most definitely rough around the edges, but she'd been kind to me since my arrival in Sinful. Granted, she had to have known that instigating a game of "Pin the Tail on the Bitch" wasn't going to end well but, in fairness, I had asked her to distract the shower guests. And that she did. I cleared my throat. "I can only repeat that I'm truly sorry, Cassandra. I know I'm not alone." When no one chimed in, I verbally nudged them. "Right, Aunt Ida Belle?"

Her head snapped up. "Oh, yeah, right. Sure. I am sorry." Her gaze settled on the plate of cookies. "Shame about the cake."

"It certainly turned into a disaster," Gertie concurred, "but take heart, honey. With the divorce rate as high as it is, you're likely to get another chance at this whole bride thing one day."

Incredulous, I could only stare. What could I follow that up with? These women were going to be the death of me. The absolute death.

"So, is the wedding off or still on?" Fortune asked. "We heard about your dad."

Well, that was certainly direct. Cassandra must have agreed because she blinked rapidly several times before she answered. "Oh, it's on. One thousand percent on. A few stray bullets aren't going to stop me from marrying Devon. In fact, that's why I'm here." She turned and laid a hand on my arm. "Stephanie, promise me you'll come to the wedding. I absolutely need you there."

It was my turn to blink. Had I heard that right? She was re-inviting us to the wedding, not disinviting us? "Of course, I want to be there for you, Cassandra, but what about my great-aunt and friends?" I knew I was about to push the envelope, but I had to. One for all and all for one. "I'll only attend if we're all invited."

A quiet few seconds passed. "If you feel so strongly, then of course you must bring your friends." Her grip on my arm tightened. "But you'll impress upon them how important my big day is to me?"

I patted her hand. "Absolutely, I will. I promise."

I'd hammer it into them if that's what I had to do.

"AUNT IDA BELLE, YOU need to let Walter hold you closer." I motioned for her to take a few steps toward him. "You cannot properly waltz if there's two feet between you."

"Says who?" she grumbled.

Gertie, sitting in a folding chair against the church basement wall, snorted. "Miss Prim and Proper, that's who. And she knows more than you do about this dancing crap. Ah, heck, everyone knows more about it than you."

"Pardon me, Kase," I said as I extricated myself from his arms. "This should only take a moment." I made a beeline for my great-aunt. Once I reached her, I laid a gentle hand on Walter's shoulder. "You're going to have to hold her closer, Walter. The man leads, so don't be hesitant." I placed my free hand on my aunt's back and moved her toward Walter. "There, now hold that stance while we practice."

"Come on, Ida Belle, it can't be all that bad to be in my arms." The twinkle in Walter's eye and his teasing tone put a blush on her cheeks and a smile on my face.

I turned to check on Fortune and Carter. In contrast to Walter and my great-aunt, they were standing indecently close. I clapped my hands. "Carter, please take a step away from Fortune. That's right. You two need to maintain a proper distance between you." I sighed. Perhaps borrowing the church basement for a last-minute dance refresher course hadn't been wise. But, based on the dancing I'd seen thus far, it had been necessary. Had these women never waltzed before? Only around the truth, would by my guess.

I rejoined Kase, feeling remarkably comfortable in his embrace despite our height difference. There was something solid and steadying in his presence. I was even growing accustomed to his snake tattoo. But, of course, this had less to do with a personal attraction than it did with my appreciating his sanity. A rare commodity in this town. "Are we ready to try again?"

Without waiting for an answer, I motioned for Gertie to hit the music. I can't speak for the other ladies, but I enjoyed the next half an hour as Kase guided me around the room. I lost myself in the rhythm of the waltz, right up until the basement door flung open and crashed into the wall. We all stopped dancing and stared at the human tornado that had just blown in.

Celia, Sinful's mayor-from-hell, stood in the door way, complete with a sour expression that would curdle milk.

"What in tarnation do you want, you old gas bag?" my great-aunt called out. "We've got this room for another thirty minutes. Now shoo."

Celia ignored her. "Carter, you unhand that bottle blonde this instant and report for duty." Celia's tone took imperious to a whole new level.

"I'm not on duty, Celia." Carter's voice was strained but still professional. "Deputy Breaux is working tonight. Have someone at the station get ahold of him."

Celia strode across the room until she stood before him. "No one else can handle this. It's an emergency."

Gertie cut the music.

Carter released his hold on Fortune and settled his hands on his hips. His face was a deferential mask. "What's so all-fired important that only I can handle it?"

"Drugs."

Kase and I exchanged a startled glance. What had Celia stumbled across that we'd missed?

"You got a drug problem? Go to rehab," Gertie said. "Take all the time you need there. We'll hold down the fort here."

Carter held up his hand before Celia could blow her top. "Drugs? What are you talking about?" His tone had changed, though. He sounded less annoyed and more alert.

"There's a drug czar here in Sinful and I want them eliminated." She waved her hand dismissively. "Arrested or shot, dead or alive, I don't care. Just get it done tonight."

"Can you give me a little something more concrete to go on?"

Celia whirled around and pointed directly at me. "Ask her. Miss Prim and Proper. She's in it up to her fancy little neck."

Instinctively, I touched my string of pearls. Kase's arm tightened around my waist. "Me?" I squeaked out.

Celia's expression was triumphant. "See, the drugs are getting to her brain already."

Gertie shot to her feet. "At least she's got a brain. More than we can say for you, Madam Straw for Brains."

Aunt Ida Belle lunged for Celia, but luckily Walter was able to grab her before she could wrap her hands around Celia's neck. Carter moved between the two women.

"Celia, you'd better hush up right now before you say something even more slanderous," Carter warned her.

"It would be a shame to see you get sued by Stephanie's hotshot Boston newspaper," Fortune said, although her tone implied the opposite. "A lawsuit like that would cost the town a pretty penny, and I bet the city council would vote your sorry butt out of office faster than you could say 'I resign.'"

"Enough." Kase's voice cut off the blow-up we all knew was coming. "Celia, I can assure you that Stephanie is the last person in Sinful who would be involved with illegal drugs. I'm going to tell you just once that you'd better not level that accusation again." He took a step toward her. "Do you need me to repeat that?"

Eyes wide, Celia shook her head. I'd never seen the woman cower in front of anyone before, but she was doing so now. I don't know if it was Kase's size or his snake tattoo that she found menacing, but she remained silent.

"Good. I'm glad you understand me. Now, what is it that you know that you think Deputy LeBlanc needs to know?"

Celia swallowed hard. "Brazilian nut."

We all exchanged confused glances.

"Come again?" Kase crossed his arms over his chest.

"I'm talking about that Brazilian woman flouncing around town today acting as high as a kite. She said she knew Ida Belle's niece."

Realization dawned. She meant Carmen. "She's Colombian, Celia, not Brazilian. And her name is Carmen."

"Whatever. I don't care. I just want her gone."

Carter blew out a long breath. "There aren't any laws in Sinful prohibiting a Colombian-born woman from visiting our town. I'd suggest you quit trying to stir up trouble before you create an international incident."

I still had no idea why Celia would implicate me in any illicit activities, but I didn't trust her to give me a straight answer, so I didn't ask. At this point, I just wanted her gone.

As if she could read my thoughts, she shook a finger in my direction. "If I catch you bringing trouble to Sinful, Miss Priss, I'll have you run out of town like the Yankee trash you are." She ignored my great-aunt's growl. "Carter, you have twenty-four hours to prove to me that there isn't a trail of drugs following that foreign woman into my town." With one last furious glance directed at each of us, she stormed out of the basement.

"Twenty-four hours?" Gertie shook her head. "Geez. Nothing like a little pressure."

"What are we going to do?" Walter asked.

"The same thing we were going to do before she blew in here," I said. "We're going to go to the wedding and find out what the Masters family is up to. I don't know just how, but I know we can do it." I took hold of Kase's hand. "Now, everyone, let's work on our Foxtrot. Gertie, cue the music, please."

Chapter Ten

I FELT AS HARRIED AS the mother of triplet toddlers as I encouraged my three companions to get ready for the wedding. I'd finished getting dressed well before the time we'd agreed on. My hair was pinned up in a chignon, my make-up was tastefully applied, and I was dressed in an ice blue shantung silk sheath dress with silver-tone heels. All I needed was one last swipe of lipstick before I was ready to walk out the door. The same could not be said for the other ladies. We'd decided the night before that Fortune and Gertie would come over to dress for the wedding at my great-aunt's house. It had seemed so very simple then.

"I don't know what you're so worked up about, Stephanie." Fortune turned to survey the reflection of her posterior in the full-length mirror. She smoothed her hands over her fitted red dress and then lifted her gaze to catch my eye. "You can't even tell I have panties on."

That was because she didn't have any on, a point that I wasn't about to debate. Ladies didn't discuss "going commando". "It's the unsightly bulge in the front of your dress that concerns me, Fortune."

She turned around and there, in all its glory, was the outline of a tiny Beretta pistol tucked into her waistband. She lifted her hands in an expression of feigned innocence. "What's wrong with accessorizing?"

My eyebrows shot up right along with my blood pressure. She was concerned about accessorizing? "You'd be better off losing the gun and finding some earrings that aren't in the shape of bananas."

Fortune reached up to touch an ear lobe, her expression defensive. "Gertie gave these to me. When else am I going to wear them?"

Before I could respond, the shrill tone of the landline rang.

"Don't get it," Gertie screamed from down the hallway. "It's bull."

I frowned. "What's bull?"

"This whole getting gussied up nonsense is bull crap if you ask me." Aunt Ida Belle sat perched on the edge of her bed. She waved a pair of nylon stockings over her head. "There's not a man alive stupid enough to wear these things, so why in the hell should I have to?" Without waiting for an answer, she stuck her finger through one leg like a defiant eight-year-old. "Aw, shucks, can't wear them now."

"Not so fast, Aunt Ida Belle." I rustled around in one of the bags from my shopping trip to New Orleans. Triumphantly, I pulled out a spare pair that I'd purchased for her. "Voila! No need to worry that you'll be forced to endure an evening with bare legs." I tossed the package to her. "Be careful, but in case you do accidentally tear them, fear not. I have several more pair in your size."

The phone rang again. Seconds later, a breathless Gertie stuck her head in the room. "Don't answer it," she panted. "It's just bull." She tore off again before anyone could question her.

"Do we need to ask what that's all about?" I asked.

"No!" Aunt Ida Belle and Fortune answered in emphatic unison.

I shrugged, deciding it was wise to pick my battles. The night was young. I glanced at my watch. "Kase is going to be here soon. Let's not keep him waiting. Fortune, please put that gun somewhere where no one will see it. Try a handbag. Aunt Ida Belle, stockings on. Take one for the team." I double-checked that I had a tissue, my cell phone, and a tube of lipstick in my clutch. "I'm off to make sure that Gertie's dressed appropriately." Something I doubted she could manage on her own. The dressing part, yes, but the appropriate part, no. "Let's meet downstairs in ten minutes."

A few minutes later, I sagged against the guest bedroom doorframe and watched as Gertie fiddled with her hat. She caught sight of me and grinned. I experienced a stab of affection for this woman I'd known such a short time. Gertie was a kind soul with an energy that I admired, and a heart of pure gold. But still, the hat had to go. "Hi, Gertie." I advanced into the room and sat on the bed. "You look lovely. That camouflage scarf goes beautifully with your dress." I wasn't a fan of camo prints, but nonetheless I thought the scarf was a much-needed pop of color against her all beige outfit. "But the pith helmet is a no go."

She cocked her head. "Really? I shouldn't wear it?"

I shook my head regretfully. "Not unless we're headed out on safari." And probably not even then.

She grinned. "That's why I chose it. You saw what a jungle that bridal shower turned into."

I'd walked right into that one. "Yes, well, that's all behind us now. Cassandra's wedding is going to be an elegant affair."

Reluctantly, Gertie tossed the hat onto the bed.

The phone rang again. "Bull."

"Why do you keep saying that?" I knew that question might well lead to a long, convoluted answer, but I was curious. Was it some sort of code for something in Sinful? "What's bull?"

Gertie winked. "My date."

"Your date is bull?"

She nodded, rather more enthusiastically than seemed warranted considering that she thought so little of the man.

"Total bull, I know," she finished for me. She grabbed her two-ton purse and slung it up on her shoulder. Her expression was eager and her eyes shone with excitement. "I'm ready to rhumba. So are you from the look of those shoes."

I glanced down at my feet. My heels were a couple of inches higher than I normally wore. I was suddenly unsure if they were appropriate for a daytime wedding. "I think I'll run upstairs and change my shoes."

Gertie grabbed my arm. "Don't you dare."

Her vehement reaction startled me. "Why ever not?"

I could have sworn a faint blush stained her cheeks, but that made no sense.

"Trust me, Kase is going to love those shoes. Don't ruin his fun." She tugged me toward the bedroom door. "Ready?"

Ready as I'd ever be.

THE ATMOSPHERE AT THE Masters home was surprisingly placid considering the number of guests milling about the grounds. You'd never have known that the bride's father had been shot at less than twenty-four hours ago. We all made our way through the house and out onto the lawn where the ceremony was going to be held.

We'd agreed on the drive over to stay in pairs throughout the evening. Fortune and Carter were paired up, Walter and Ida Belle, Kase and I, and Gertie and Bull. Yes, Bull, Gertie's date. Bull Dozer, all five-foot-two inches and ninety-eight pounds of him, showed up at my great-aunt's house just as we were about to leave. Between his shock of red hair and baby blue tuxedo, I hardly knew what to make of him. I watched him out of the corner of my eye as he brought Gertie a glass of champagne. "He seems sweet enough."

"Don't be fooled," my great-aunt grumbled. "He's a man just like any other. No sense of loyalty."

Kase and I exchanged amused glances. Aunt Ida Belle was in a foul mood, which I attributed to the fact that Lenora Masters had whisked Walter away the moment we'd arrived. Deep down she cared about Walter, I knew she did. I also knew she'd be darned before she'd admit it.

"Do you want me to drag him back here?" Kase asked.

I smiled up at him. I was quickly growing to appreciate his subtle sense of humor. Aunt Ida Belle, however, showed no such inclination. Her face took on the look of a summer thunderstorm.

"Like hell you will." She downed an entire glass of champagne in one gulp before thrusting her crystal glass at a passing waiter. "If Walter needs straightening out, then I'm the woman for the job." She squared her shoulders, patted her hair into place, and strode off in the direction we'd last seen Walter and Lenora.

Now that we were alone, I turned my attention to Kase. I'd never seen him dressed in formalwear before. He wore a gray suit, a white button-down Oxford shirt, and a light purple tie. The cut of his suit suggested that he'd had it tailor made, and he wore it with ease equal to his regular t-shirt and jeans. The biggest surprise when he'd picked me up, though, hadn't been what he was wearing, but rather what he was missing. He'd cut his hair short. It was a good look on him, and I told him so in a jumbled rush of embarrassed words.

I took a sip of champagne and gazed around, doing my level best to look anywhere but at Kase. No easy task, I must admit, especially when I could feel his eyes on me. I blushed. "Aren't you supposed to be looking for someone who's up to their neck in narcotics?" I asked, unable to resist peeking up at him.

"Yes, I am, but you are so beautiful that I'm struggling to look anywhere but at you." He took a step closer and brushed a tendril of my hair back from my cheek. "When I picked you up at your aunt's house and I saw you in that dress, you took my breath away. I'm still recovering."

His compliment pleased me, but it also left me feeling self-conscious. Time for a change of subject. "Maybe we should split up and circulate."

Kase shook his head. "It's better if we stay together. After all, the Masters know me as your bodyguard. Stands to reason I'd be right beside you. Besides, there's precious little we can do other than watch and listen. Carter's called in backup from the DEA to watch a few key landing points where possible shipments could come in." He glanced down at his watch. "The ceremony should start soon anyway."

As if on cue from a stage manager, the mother-of-the-bride appeared at our side. She looked even more flustered than usual. "Miss St. James, I'm so sorry to bother you, but I need your help," she said in a breathless rush of words.

"Is something amiss?"

She nodded. "It's Cassandra. She just texted me." She looked around nervously. "She's distraught. I need your help to calm her down."

"Of course, I'd be happy to help if I'm able. Is she getting cold feet?"

Kitty stared at me for a long moment as if she were trying to decipher my question. "Oh, no, goodness no," she finally said. "Nothing like that. It's, well, it's her father."

Kase and I exchanged baffled looks. As per most situations in Sinful, this conversation wasn't making much sense.

"Is he drunk?" Kase asked.

Kitty clasped her hands together. "Worse."

What could be worse than a drunk father-of-the-bride? That was about as bad as it got in my book. "Is he ill?" I asked.

"I wish. No, he's missing."

"Late, you mean?" Kase asked.

"No, missing. As in a no-show." It was as if a dark shadow passed over her face. "Can you please come upstairs with me, Miss St. James?"

Nodding, I moved to follow her, but Kase's grip on my elbow prevented me from taking more than a step.

"If Miss St. James is going to accompany you, so am I," Kase said, his voice resolute. "I trust that won't be a problem."

Kitty didn't meet his eye. "That's fine, but let's go. The harpist will start playing soon and my little girl is freaking out."

Kase did his best to muscle us through the throng of guests, but every few steps Kitty was stopped by someone who wanted to compliment her dress, exchange air kisses, or ask where the soon-to-be newlyweds were going for their honeymoon. After a few moments, Kitty leaned in and whispered, "Just go ahead without me. Cassandra's in the room at the top of the stairs, the first door on the right. I'll be along as soon as I can."

I could tell Kase wasn't thrilled with leaving Kitty behind, but he parted the seas for me and we were inside the house within minutes. I looked over my shoulder but couldn't see her head in the crowd. She wasn't where we'd left her.

"Do you think we should wait for Kitty?" I asked Kase.

He looked around. His height afforded him a far better view than I had. Once he'd completed his surveillance, he shook his head. "I don't see her. Let's go."

We made it as far as the foyer, but as I stepped foot on the staircase, we heard a blood-curdling scream from the landing above.

Chapter Eleven

SHOCK RIPPLED THROUGH my body like a streak of lightning, but it didn't stop me from bolting up the stairs. I moved quickly enough to elude Kase's attempt to hold me back. I also ignored his shouted orders to come down and wait with the guests. He could stay downstairs if he wanted, and he could call 911 while he was at it, because based on the screams I was hearing, someone had been badly hurt.

Make that shot. Possibly killed, judging by the amount of blood that had escaped Donny Master's chest cavity. He lay in the middle of the upstairs landing. I stopped short, grateful to feel the solid weight of Kase's chest as I took a step backward.

"Dios mio, he's dead." Carmen sank to her knees beside her husband's body. Her English gave way to Spanish, but it wasn't hard to translate her keening. She ignored Kase's command to not touch her husband. She grabbed Donny's hand.

Kase shoved his cell phone into my hand as he moved past me. "Call 911, get an ambulance. Then call Carter and tell him what happened. Don't let anyone up the stairs unless it's the paramedics or law enforcement." Once he'd barked orders at me, he crossed the landing, pulled a sobbing Carmen from her husband's body, and knelt beside Donny.

My hands shook as I dialed for help, and I felt lost in a fog as I gave the operator the information she needed. I watched as Kase checked for Donny's pulse. It didn't escape my notice that he wasn't attending to Donny's gunshot wound. Hardly an encouraging sign.

The door to my right flew open. Cassandra, in all of her bridal finery, stepped into the hallway. "For God's sake, Carmen, be quiet—" but her angry protest died on her lips as she took in the scene in front of her. She sagged against the doorframe. "Oh, my God, what happened?"

"Don't move," Kase ordered her. "Stay where you are." He turned to meet my eye. "You made those calls?" His voice was barely audible above Cassandra's panicked cries.

I nodded, but I was unable to form words. I shifted my attention to a sobbing Carmen. I should go to her. I should do something, say something, but I felt paralyzed.

"Stay where you are, Stephanie," Kase instructed me as if he could read my frantic thoughts. "I need you to keep your eyes on the stairs."

Again, I nodded. My eyes swept over the scene. I didn't see a gun, so whomever shot Donny must have taken it with them. Unless...oh, no, it couldn't be. I stared at Carmen in horror. Had she shot her husband? Was her behavior that of a shocked wife or a murderess? Her dress was a dark navy-blue chiffon, and if there was any of her husband's blood on it, I couldn't tell.

Cassandra's piteous cries of "Daddy, Daddy" were painful to hear. But were they sincere? Was she shocked to see that her father had been shot? Or was her reaction a clever cover for a premeditated act?

"Lord almighty!"

I whirled around. Gertie stood on the step below me, her eyes wide.

"Oh, Gertie, thank goodness you're here." I reached out for her hand. "We need Carter."

She stared at Donny's still form. "What you need is a miracle."

That too.

Kase got to his feet. "Gertie, have Bull stand at the bottom of the stairs and not let anyone up here except Carter and the paramedics. They should be here soon." As he spoke, the sound of approaching sirens reached our ears.

"Will do," Gertie said. She turned and had a word with her date, who nodded and hustled down the stairs. "Where's Lenora?" she asked me.

Good God. I hadn't thought about Donny's step-mother. "Isn't she with Walter and Aunt Ida Belle?"

Gertie shook her head. "Last I saw Ida Belle she was madder than a hornet because Walter slipped away with Lenora when she went to fetch a drink. You want me to go look for them?"

The arrival of the paramedics cut off any further conversation. Gertie and I stepped aside as they swept up the stairs. Within moments of their arrival, the swell of wedding guests that had been awaiting the ceremony out on the lawn somehow squeezed into the house. I peered down the stairs. It appeared as if Bull Dozer was struggling to keep anyone from coming up the stairs. Deputy Breaux was attempting to herd guests back outside.

Carter jogged up the stairs, nodding to us as he made his way to where the paramedics were kneeling over Donny's body. He and Kase spoke in such low tones that I couldn't make out their actual words, but it was obvious that while Donny's body was still here, his soul had departed this earth. The paramedics would soon leave and someone from the coroner's office would come in instead. The landing would transform from a death scene to a crime scene.

"Donny?" The bewildered voice of his first wife floated up the stairway. "Stephanie, what's going on? Has Donny shown up yet?"

My stomach clenched. Oh, yes, he'd come. And gone. But I couldn't find my voice.

Luckily, Gertie had no such problem. "Bull, honey, let Kitty come on up."

Kitty ran lightly up the stairs. "Is Donny here? Is he drunk?" She stopped next to Gertie. From the angle where we stood the only part of her ex-husband that was visible were the bottoms of his black dress shoes. "He's passed out drunk, isn't he?" Her hands clenched by her side, and she shook with a barely contained rage. "I knew he'd find a way to ruin Cassandra's day, the bastard. I'm going to kill him."

But as the words left her lips, the paramedics moved away from Donny's body, showing Kitty Masters that she wasn't the first person that day to have the same idea.

AN HOUR LATER WE WERE gathered at the police station. Carter looked weary and Kase looked worried. Donny's body had been taken to the morgue, and the former and current Mrs. Donny Masters sat in separate meeting rooms giving their statements to deputies. Cassandra and her fiancé were at the hospital at Shawn's bedside waiting to see if he'd recover from an overdose. Carter and Kase had their heads together conferring over notes while Fortune, Gertie, and I loitered in the police station hallway like law enforcement groupies.

"I don't like this," Fortune said. "Not one bit."

I shot an annoyed look in her direction. "Really? The rest of us are having so much fun."

Gertie frowned. "Don't start, either one of you. It's not going to help us figure out where Ida Belle is."

And this was the crux of our problem. Somehow, in the melee at the Masters house, we'd lost my great-aunt, Walter, and Lenora. So far as we knew, Lenora had no idea her step-son had been killed. We were anxious to get word to her before she heard it from someone else. One of the sheriff's deputies who was at the hospital keeping an eye on Cassandra and Shawn was under strict orders to let us know if Lenora showed up at the hospital.

"Could the three of them have gone off to hash things out?" I suggested.

"Bash it out would be more like it," Gertie said. "Last I saw of Ida Belle, she was madder than a wet hen on a hot tin roof."

I was too tired to point out the absurdity of her metaphor. "Could they have been kidnapped by the murderer?"

Fortune shrugged. "To what end? Whoever pulled the trigger would be desperate to get out of there. You can't move fast when you're hustling hostages around."

I watched her carefully. She was nervous, which did nothing to reassure me. Her pensive expression told me what her words didn't. She thought that the three missing seniors had met the same fate as Donny. But she couldn't be right. Aunt Ida Belle couldn't be dead. Not now, not like this.

"Maybe it was the wife," Gertie suggested.

"Which one?" Fortune asked.

Gertie threw up her hands. "Either one, I don't have a preference. Maybe the newer model? She was upstairs when you and Mayeux got up there, wasn't she?"

I nodded. "Yes, leaning over her husband's body."

"Did you see a gun?" Fortune asked.

"I don't know. I don't think so. If Kase had, he'd have pointed it out to Carter." I squeezed my eyes shut and tried to replay the scene in my mind. I shook my head. "I can't remember any details. All I could see was the blood on Donny's shirt." I crossed my hands over my stomach, willing it not to retch. "There was so much blood. Maybe Carmen hid the gun before we got upstairs. I'm sorry."

"Don't be hard on yourself," Fortune said. "It takes years of practice to learn to assess a crime scene."

Years? Perhaps this was true for the Queen of Delusion, but I could never get used to seeing freshly murdered bodies. I certainly couldn't speak about it so dispassionately.

Gertie reached out and laid a hand on my shoulder. "Try one more time, kiddo. Tell us everything you remember from the moment you last saw Ida Belle. Don't over-think it, just talk."

I nodded. "Okay. After you and Bull left us, Kase and I stood on the lawn with Aunt Ida Belle. She was distressed that Lenora had spirited Walter away. Kase offered to go find him but that just set her off."

Gertie snorted. "I can see it."

"She then took off toward the house, but I didn't watch her. She might have gone into the house or in another direction. I don't know. I feel so stupid for not paying more attention."

"Don't be silly, honey. If you hadn't been enjoying the day with your man, you'd have been wasting precious time," Gertie said.

Kase wasn't my man, but this wasn't the time to set Gertie straight. We could do that after we found Aunt Ida Belle. "Kase and I talked for a few moments more, and then Kitty came up to us and asked for my help. She said that Donny hadn't shown up and that she wanted me to help calm Cassandra down. I agreed to accompany her to the house."

"How did Kitty seem?" Gertie said. "Maybe she shot Donny and then rushed out to get you and Kase so she could lead you upstairs and act stunned with the two of you as witnesses."

I shook my head. "I don't think so. She appeared flustered, but that seems normal for her."

"How did she act when she saw the body?" Fortune asked.

I shrugged. "She didn't go upstairs with us. On the way to the house so many people stopped her that she suggested we go ahead without her. She said she'd be right along."

"Odd that she'd stop to talk to guests at a time like that," Fortune said.

"It's not odd at all," I disagreed. "It was the only polite thing for a hostess to do."

"Ida Belle needs our help." Gertie said. "I can feel it in my old bones."

Her concern for my great-aunt was so palpable that tears filled my eyes. Gertie was easy to make fun of, easy to tease or dismiss as wacky, but she was a dear and loyal friend to Aunt Ida Belle. I wrung my hands. "What are we going to do?"

"We're going to find them, that's what we're going to do." Gertie rubbed her hands together, a determined look on her face. "Ida Belle would come looking for us, wouldn't she?"

Neither Fortune nor I dignified this with an answer. Of course she would come after us, guns blazing, of this I had no doubt.

"That's settled. We're going after her." Gertie grabbed her purse. "C'mon."

"Wait," I protested, "We don't know where she is."

Gertie grinned. "We'll figure it out on the way there. Let's roll."

Chapter Twelve

"DO YOU THINK THEY BOUGHT it?" I asked from the backseat of Gertie's Cadillac.

Fortune, who was riding shotgun, checked the car's side mirror. "We're clear. No one's following us. Carter will be tied up for a while yet with filing reports, so don't worry about him. Your boyfriend, however, will hunt us down if he thinks we're up to something."

"Doesn't matter," Gertie said. She swerved wildly to avoid a pothole. "By the time he figures out we lied to him, we'll have found Ida Belle and Walter."

From her lips to God's ears. I, however, didn't share her confidence that we'd outrun Kase if he decided to come after us. But hopefully he and Carter were still at the station waiting for us to return. They'd had the audacity to question our intentions when we told them we were going to pick up sandwiches and apple pie to bring back to them. At first, it didn't look like they were buying it, but the thought of Ally's baking must have tipped the scales in our favor. Their complete lack of trust that we were headed where we said we were would have been downright insulting if they hadn't been right.

I clung to the seat in front of me. Gertie was tearing up the road as if she knew exactly where she was going. "Where are we going? Back to the Masters home?"

"Nope. Still haven't heard squat from Bull, which means he hasn't seen hide nor hair of anyone."

"What if Bull's in on it?" I asked.

Gertie slammed on the brakes. New York City cabbies had nothing on this woman. Luckily, I already had a grip on the back of her seat, so the whiplash wasn't too painful.

She slipped the Caddy into park and twisted around to face me. "What did you just say?"

I'd never seen her so irate. "We don't know Bull very well. In fact, if I'm not mistaken, you're the only one who knew him before tonight." My words sounded more accusatory than I meant them to, but I didn't think we should eliminate Bull Dozer from suspicion just because Gertie was sweet on him.

Gertie's eyes narrowed. "Those are fighting words, Miss Prim and Proper."

"Stop, stop, stop." Fortune's words were laced with frustration. "Fighting about a man isn't going to help Ida Belle, so just can it. Gertie, turn around and drive."

Once we were back to racing down the dirt road, Gertie spoke again. "Bull's not our guy."

Her confident tone implied she had someone else in mind. "So, who is then?" I asked.

"Lenora Masters."

"What?" I didn't just hear that.

"She may be right," Fortune said. "Think about it. Who's the most unlikely member of the Masters family to be behind something like this?"

I groaned aloud. "Honestly, Fortune. This isn't a mystery novel. We're talking about a real murder, not a whodunit with a colorful cast of characters. This is real life, and little old ladies are very often what they appear to be. Quiet. Shy. Retiring, as well as retired." My gaze flitted to Gertie. "With a few notable exceptions, of course. But my point is that not everyone sees life through the same distorted lens that you apparently do."

"Holy crap, you've done it now, Stephanie." Gertie shook her head. "Fortune, let it go. Remember that she's just a wee babe in terms of having seen the world."

"No, Gertie, don't sugarcoat this," I said. "Fortune, I respect that as a librarian you've read hundreds of books, but this is reality. Aunt Ida Belle, Walter, and Lenora are in real trouble. Gertie and I need you to stay focused."

Fortune's response was a string of unladylike expletives that I wouldn't repeat even if someone put a gun to my head.

"If you two young'uns don't stop bickering, I'm going to pull over, let you out, and you can walk back to town." Gertie hit the accelerator, which catapulted us near into light speed.

"Where are we going?" Fortune asked before I could, but I wanted to know the same thing. Clearly, Gertie had a destination in mind.

"Walter's fishing cabin."

Again with a cabin? Was there some unwritten law in Sinful that every crisis required a visit to an isolated cabin? When Boris Sidorov kidnapped me several weeks ago, he'd ordered his henchmen to deliver me to an old hunting cabin where he'd intended to kill me. Luckily, Aunt Ida Belle, Gertie, and Fortune had busted in to save me. Then, just about a week ago, Fortune and I had taken a trip to Number Two and found Boris and one of his thugs hiding in yet another cabin. Fortune had blown out both of Boris' kneecaps, so that had ended well, at least for us, but now we were going for a threepeat?

"We're wasting precious time, Gertie," I said. Not that I had any better idea where we should begin to look, but I just couldn't buy that they were at Walter's cabin. "For all we know, they were whisked onto a boat and they're out in the middle of the bayou somewhere." I shivered, and not because it was chilly. "Lenora can't be the one who's behind this."

"Why not?" Fortune challenged me. "And don't give me this 'old ladies don't kill' crap either."

"Lenora would hardly have killed her own step-child," I shot back. "Think about it, Fortune. Someone shot that man straight in the chest and they were aiming to kill. Hardly the work of a mother figure."

"Prisons are full of women who've killed their children, Stephanie. Give me a real reason that Lenora isn't the one behind all of this."

"Why on earth would she get involved with drug trafficking? She has a lovely home—"

"Which could have been provided for with drug money," Fortune interrupted me. "You've got to admit that she's erratic and displays some bizarre behavior at times."

True, but I could well say that about most of the people in Sinful. Lenora Masters wasn't any crazier than anyone else who called this town home.

"Hush up, now, both of you." Gertie slowed the car and turned off the lights. "We're almost there." The Cadillac rolled to a stop and Gertie cut the engine. She turned to look at us. "I know Lenora's going to kill Walter and frame Ida Belle for murder unless we stop her."

WITH GERTIE IN THE lead, Fortune and I crept along behind her as we approached the cabin. I didn't see a car, but it could well be hidden. A small golden light glowed through the closed curtains.

"Wait," I hissed. I grabbed hold of Gertie's elbow so that she'd stop walking. "What if we're interrupting?"

"That's the whole point, kiddo. We want to get to Lenora before she kills Walter."

"No, that's not what I meant." I leaned in and lowered my voice. "What if Walter and Aunt Ida Belle are here in a—" how to put this delicately? "—romantic capacity?"

Both Fortune and Gertie stared at me for a full minute before they rolled their eyes in perfect synchronicity. Fortune shook her head. "Trust me, that isn't what's going on in there, Stephanie. At this point we're just going to have to trust Gertie's intuition. She's known Lenora far longer than we have."

Frustration welled up within me. I was certain that they were barking up the wrong tree. But how to convince them? "I'm one hundred percent sure that Lenora is as innocent in all of this as Aunt Ida Belle is. I'm so sure that I'd bet my pearls that Gertie's wrong."

Instead of answering me, Fortune cupped her hands together and put them in front of her mouth. She let out an ear-splitting imitation of an owl.

"Good thinking," Gertie whispered. "You finish that up and I'll sneak around front."

I watched her go with more than a little trepidation. "Finish what up?"

Fortune changed the position of her hands and emitted another unearthly sound.

"Finish what up?" I asked again. "Fortune, what are you doing?"

She dropped her hands. "Sending a signal to Ida Belle that the cavalry's here. Let me finish."

I waited while she repeated the owl sound and then added another bird call. What was this? Some sort of avian Morse code?

"Okay, let's go," Fortune said when she was finished.

"Wait, I don't know what we're doing," I protested. My heart was hammering in my chest. "What's the plan?"

Fortune met my eye. "Look, Stephanie, maybe you should wait in the car." She held up a hand when I started to object. "That way you can call for help if something goes wrong."

"Something? Try everything's going wrong." I heard the high-pitched squeal that my voice had morphed into but Fortune's calm unnerved me. Wait in the car? What was I? A Labrador? "I think we should call for help now."

"Good idea." Fortune glanced over her shoulder in the direction of the Cadillac. "Head over to the car, call for help, and then give us five to seven minutes to wrap this up. That's all the time we'll need."

Before I could object, she sprinted toward the cabin. I confess that I uttered a most unladylike curse, however if any situation ever called for blue language, I believed this was it. The only reasonable course of action was to call for help. I jogged back to the car where I'd left my cell phone, hoping against hope that I could get some sort of signal this far out of town.

Which, of course, I couldn't. I shook my phone, held it up above my head, turned it to the left and to the right, and then did the whole hokey-pokey reception dance, but nothing brought forth a single bar. Disgusted, I tossed the phone back into the Cadillac.

I took a dozen steps toward the cabin before I froze. Behind me, no more than twenty feet at most, was the unmistakable sound of a gigantic creature crunching through the underbrush. I squeezed my eyes shut. I issued a silent prayer that it would turn around and run the other way. Fast. But instead, the sounds came closer. For the first time ever, I wished I were packing more than just lipstick and a tissue in my handbag. "Go away," I cried. Although I heard the anguish in my voice, I doubted that whatever manner of beast this was would care about my fear. I buried my face in my hands and waited for it to pounce.

The pounce came, but it was in the form of two large arms wrapping themselves around my waist. I let out a whoosh of pent up oxygen that I'd been saving for my last scream on earth when I recognized the scent of Kase's cologne.

He pulled me back close against his chest. "Unless Ally has opened a bakery here in the woods, you've got some serious explaining to do."

Chapter Thirteen

I DIDN'T WASTE PRECIOUS time apologizing for misleading Kase. Nor did I ask how he found us—time for that explanation later. The only thing that mattered now was filling him on the girls' wild idea that Lenora Masters was the one who was behind the drug trafficking and the kidnapping. But after my words tumbled out in a rush, he didn't reject their theory.

Instead, he frowned. "Well, I'll be damned. And Gertie's sure about this?"

I nodded.

"Fortune's on board?" he asked.

"Yes, but I'm not about to give credence to her wild ideas. Her grasp on reality is tenuous at best."

He narrowed his eyes. "You're sure?"

I reached up and touched my necklace. "Sure enough that I bet my pearls on it."

He drew his hand down over his face. "Where are Gertie and Fortune now?"

I pointed toward the cabin. "They wanted me to call for help, but I couldn't get a signal."

Kase furrowed his brow. "Wait here while I call for backup." He took a few steps away from me but then doubled back to put a hand under my elbow. "Better yet, come with me." He led me back to his truck and insisted I sit in the cab while he phoned in to the station.

"Tell them it's Walter's cabin. Carter will know the way here."

Kase relayed the information and then shoved the phone in his pocket. "I want you to wait here."

Acquiescence made complete sense, but instead I got out of the truck and moved a few feet away from him. "Aunt Ida Belle needs me."

"Needs you to stay safe, yes, you're right on that point." He reached into his truck and pulled out a pair of handcuffs.

I gasped. "You wouldn't dare."

In answer, he took a menacing step toward me.

"Kase Mayeux, get that idea right out of your head." I took several steps backward without taking my eyes off him. "Aren't you supposed to be savings someone's life right now?"

"Don't get smart with me."

Smart? The only smart thing to do was to get moving before he cuffed me to his truck. So, I did. I sprinted toward Walter's cabin. I reached the door before Kase, and I didn't stop to think. I flung open the door and stumbled right into a nightmarish scene.

Walter sat slumped in a chair smack in the middle of the cabin. Fresh blood stained his white dress shirt, the red in stark contrast to the gray pallor of his skin. "Oh, my God, Walter." I rushed over and dropped to my knees beside him. "Who did this to you?"

He lifted his head and looked straight into my eyes. His breath was labored. "Ida Belle," he managed to half-whisper.

I sat back on my heels. Good heavens, he was in worse shape than I thought if he was hallucinating. My great-aunt would never, *never*, hurt Walter. She loved him, and even if she didn't want to act on her feelings for whatever reason, we all knew it to be true.

He sucked in a deep, shuddering breath. "Help Ida Belle. Please."

"Oh, Walter, you love her." Tears stung the back of my eyes. He wasn't blaming her. He was worried for her. "I will, but we need to get you help first. Where were you shot?" There was so much blood it was hard to tell.

He tried to lift his right arm but he grimaced. "Left shoulder."

"Help's on the way," I told him. I got to my feet and looked around. I needed a clean piece of fabric to press against his wound. No one else appeared to be here, but that couldn't be right. Where were Aunt Ida Belle and Lenora? Where were Gertie and Fortune?

More to the point, where in the world was Kase? He'd been right behind me.

"Oh, my dear child, you shouldn't have come."

At the sound of Lenora's voice, I whirled around. She stood in the cabin's only interior doorway. "Mrs. Masters, thank goodness you're safe." I rushed to her side. "Help me find something clean to use as a compress on Walter's wound."

Lenora looked up at me, her blue eyes unreadable. Her hands shook. "Are you here alone?"

The poor woman, she was obviously in shock. "Help's coming," I repeated what I'd told Walter.

She shook her head. "That's not good."

I glanced around the cabin, looking for another chair so she could sit. I'd ask the paramedics to examine her as soon as they'd helped Walter. "Why aren't there more chairs?" I wondered aloud. A farmhouse table stood in one corner.

"We're using them."

"Who's using the other chairs?" Uneasiness began to creep over me. It was too quiet in here. "Where's my great-aunt?"

She stepped to the side and swept her arm in the direction of the doorway that she'd just come through as if she were a museum docent giving a grand tour of a stately home. "See for yourself."

I heard the cabin's front doorknob squeak as someone on the outside ever so slowly twisted it. Judging by Lenora's expression, I doubted she'd heard it. It was Kase, and he was about to barrel into the cabin. I bit my lip. Even though I didn't see a gun on Lenora's person, someone had shot Walter. The sickening realization that Gertie had been right about Lenora crept over me. I struggled to keep my emotions from my face. What I needed to do was distract Lenora so that Kase could get in without being shot.

"Lenora, let me help get you out of here before the kidnappers come back." I took a few tentative steps toward her so as not to spook her. "We can get help for Walter as soon as you're safe."

Her wrinkled face grimaced as if I'd just offered her a glass of apple cider vinegar. "Walter doesn't want my help. He's never wanted anything from me." The look she shot him was filled with pure malice. "The only woman he's ever wanted is that crass, tacky, two-bit whore, Ida Belle."

I strove to keep my tone of voice soothing. "Walter does care about you, Lenora. All we need to do is get his shoulder looked at and then we'll sit down and he can tell you that himself."

She shook her head emphatically. "I've done everything I could over the years to show him that I was the only woman in the world for him. I agreed to work with my idiot granddaughter on this whole cocaine nonsense to make enough money to buy Walter what he deserved. A new boat, a new store, anything he wanted. But he wouldn't take a thing. I offered him the world but all he wanted was Ida Belle." Her face crumpled. "What else could I do but shoot him?"

If I lived four consecutive lifetimes I knew I couldn't answer that question. Perhaps telling her that her step-son had been killed would pierce through her obsession with Walter. "Lenora, I'm so sorry to have to tell you this, but Donny's been shot."

"Donny? Really?"

Merciful heavens, the only thing that could justify her dispassionate response was shock. Yes, that's what it must be. Shock. I nodded. "Yes, your step-son, Donny. He's been badly hurt." I couldn't make myself tell her the horrible truth.

"Hurt? Not dead?" Lenora shook her head ruefully. "She said she was going to kill him. I didn't figure her to be such a chicken."

This was taking Sinful craziness to a whole new level. I glanced at Walter, the poor man looked as if he were only half conscious. I didn't know what else to do but keep her talking until Kase got here. "Her? You mean Carmen?"

She shook her head. "Not Carmen, Cassandra. Donny threatened to turn her into the authorities if she didn't put a stop to the trafficking."

Cassandra? Good God, I hadn't seen that coming. "You're telling me that your granddaughter shot her father?"

"Step-granddaughter."

Well, this hardly seemed the time to split hairs. Where in the name of God was Kase?

"You needn't look so horrified, Stephanie. She's a very determined girl."

Well, that was one word for her. A murdering bitch was the word choice I would have run with.

"Did she do away with her brother?" Lenora asked.

I felt sick in the presence of such cold-blooded cruelty. "What do you mean?"

She glanced at her dainty wrist-watch as if to check if it were time for tea. "I imagine Shawn should have over-dosed by now."

I flinched as I heard the front door hinges creak, but I didn't indicate that I'd heard anything. Obviously, Lenora hadn't. But once Kase opened the door, she'd see the light streaming in. The idea that she could possibly get a shot off at Kase terrified me. I couldn't let that happen. I had to stop her. "Oh, Lenora, I'm so terribly sorry. I feel your pain."

Now that I was within arm's reach of her, I laid a tentative hand on her shoulder. When she didn't flinch, I mustered what little courage I possessed and grabbed the back of her three-strand pearl choker. Lenora made a horrible gagging sound as I twisted it. Her hands flew to her neck. She clawed at her choker as I pushed her to her knees.

"Stephanie, get her down flat." Kase was suddenly beside me, his weapon drawn. "Good, that's right. Keep a tight hold on her while I restrain her." In what was obviously a much-practiced move, he dropped to one knee and singlehandedly cuffed Lenora, all the while keeping his gun trained on her. He rose and helped me to my feet. "Great job, darlin.'"

The look in his eyes was so admiring that I would have loved to have basked in the warmth of his approval, but there wasn't time. Instead, I pointed to Walter.

"I'll see to him," he said. "The paramedics will be here any minute. Start looking for your aunt." He motioned to the open door with his head.

I headed straight for the second room, more than a little afraid of what I'd find. My eyes widened in shock when I stepped in the room.

Chapter Fourteen

THERE, GAGGED AND TIED to three chairs as if they were three little bears, sat Aunt Ida Belle, Gertie, and Fortune. Their expressions were a mixture of outrage, embarrassment, and resentment.

"Kase has Lenora cuffed," I told them as I whipped off their gags. "The paramedics are on their way." I untied Aunt Ida Belle first and helped her to her feet. She pulled me toward her in a brief but ferocious hug. "Walter?" she asked, her voice cracking.

I squeezed her arm. "He'll be fine. Go on, I'm sure Kase will let you ride to the hospital with him." When she was gone, I turned my attention to a now sheepish-looking Fortune and Gertie. I cocked my head to the side. "Is the five to seven minutes up yet? Wasn't that how long you said you needed to handle the situation?"

"Gloat later, kiddo." Gertie strained against her ties. "I don't want to miss what's going on out there."

Clearly, the only thing wrong with these two was a pair of badly bruised egos. I circled their chairs. "What happened? Did Lenora jump you both? At the same time? How'd she simultaneously tie you up?" I really shouldn't enjoy this so much, but I confess I was. "I just can't figure it out."

"Don't mess with me, Stephanie," Fortune growled. "Untie me."

I tugged at the ropes around Gertie's wrists. "You don't want Carter seeing you like this? I totally understand. How would a federal agent of the United States Government possibly explain how she'd been overpowered by an octogenarian?"

Gertie rubbed at her wrists before she bent down to untie her ankle restraints. "Okay, you've had your fun, Stephanie. But you've got to promise not to tell anyone that you found Fortune and me tied up. Not a soul. Ever."

"On one condition."

Fortune's frown was thunderous. "What?"

I reached up and touched my necklace. "Even though you and Gertie were right about Lenora, I was the one to take her down. Therefore, I want to keep my pearls."

"Fine, whatever," Fortune grumbled. "I didn't want the blasted thing anyway. Untie me."

I did. When we stepped into the cabin's main room, we saw Walter being wheeled out on a gurney. Aunt Ida Belle was beside him, and a hugely relieved-looking Carter stood talking to Kase. I was buzzing with an adrenaline rush that lasted throughout the evening.

ONCE WE WERE BACK HOME and seated around Aunt Ida Belle's kitchen table, however, exhaustion settled in. We were all safe, although we were collectively reeling from the news that Cassandra had confessed to her father's murder. Lenora was in the jail cell next to her granddaughter, facing charges of drug trafficking as well as kidnapping. Word at the hospital was that Shawn would likely recover from his near-fatal overdose. Kitty had confessed to throwing a gun she'd found in Shawn's room into the lake because she'd been afraid that her son had tried to kill his father. Which of course, he hadn't. His sister had pulled the trigger.

What kind of charges Kitty was going to face for interfering with an on-going police investigation, I didn't know. Once he recovered, Shawn would be charged for his part in the drug ring, although I knew he needed a trip to rehab more than a stint in jail. With the exception of Donny's widow, Carmen, the entire Masters family faced quite a bit of jail time. Talk about family bonding.

What really mattered, though, was the news that Walter's gunshot wound hadn't been nearly as bad as it had looked, and he was expected to make a full recovery.

I shook my head. "I can't wrap my mind around the idea that Cassandra killed her father. And on her wedding day?"

Gertie shrugged. "Can't explain crazy."

"Carter said she's acting as cool as a cucumber," Fortune said. "She obviously takes after her step-grandmother more than her mother."

"How much do you think Kitty knew about the drugs?" I asked.

Aunt Ida Belle cocked an eyebrow. "She may say she only suspected but I'm not buying. I believe Carmen was clueless and that Donny was the last to know, but Kitty knew something was going on. I can't prove it, but I'd bet my last bottle of beer I'm right." She turned her attention to me, a frown knitting her brows together. "Now, let's just get this over with. Why aren't you questioning why you found us tied up?"

"First I'd like to understand why you left the house with her when the wedding was about to start."

"She faked chest pains and Walter bought it," Ida Belle said. "I saw through it, but I decided to tag along to the hospital because I thought she was up to something. She pulled a gun on us once we were on the road."

"If I were you," Gertie said, "I'd be mocking all of us until the sun comes up tomorrow."

I shrugged. "I simply assumed that Lenora overpowered you."

Fortune dropped her head into her hands with an embarrassed moan.

"Well, she didn't," Aunt Ida Belle snapped. "So you can get that fool notion out of your head."

I dunked an oatmeal raisin cookie in my coffee. "I don't see why you're all so upset. It could happen to anyone."

My great-aunt's only answer was a growl.

"Remember in the car how I told you that I feared that Lenora planned to frame Ida Belle for Walter's murder?" Gertie asked me.

I nodded.

"One summer, when we were in our early twenties, the Mudbug library offered a creative writing class. Lenora and I both took the class. One of our assignments was to write a short story about a murder. I read Lenora's story, and that was it in a nutshell. Sure, she changed the names, but it was clear that the main character was Lenora, and the man who was killed was Walter. His true love was framed by the main character, and even though she was innocent she was sent to prison for his murder."

My head was spinning. "And this got you and Fortune tied up how exactly?"

Fortune blew out a long breath. "We crawled in through the window and found Lenora with a gun at Ida Belle's temple."

My stomach dropped. Poor Aunt Ida Belle.

"Gertie and I were both afraid that Lenora would kill one or both of us and find a way to make Ida Belle look guilty." She glanced at my great-aunt. "And I know Ida Belle well enough to know that she'd rather lose her life than her freedom."

"Lenora Masters may not have murdered her step-son, but she's a mad cow." Aunt Ida Belle pushed her coffee cup away. "I just want to forget the whole thing. I'm heading back to the hospital. Don't wait up for me."

Gertie grinned. "Going to spend the night with lover boy? Because we could whip you up a sexy nurse's outfit."

"Can it, Gertie. Nothing's changed between Walter and me. I'm just concerned that those young nurses are scribbling on his chart in crayon." She stood. "Someone's got to keep an eye on him. Seeing as Carter's busy at the station, I volunteered."

"Give him a kiss from us." Gertie lifted her hand and blew a loud smooch.

I shook my head as a smile stretched across my face. Gertie, bless her, just couldn't help herself. She, too, got to her feet. "I'm going to catch up with Bull. You want a ride, Fortune? I'm guessing you'll want to check in on Carter."

I was relieved when Fortune accepted the offer. She and I were going to have to work out the issues between us, but I'm sure neither one of us was in the mood tonight. I also wanted a chance to talk to Aunt Ida Belle about Fortune sometime very soon. My gut instinct told me she knew something about Fortune that I didn't, something that I needed to know if I was ever going to understand her. Besides, Kase had texted to say he was coming over and I wanted some time to make myself presentable. I waved the girls off, promising to meet up with them at Francine's in the morning for an early breakfast.

Kase arrived just as I'd applied a light stroke of lip gloss. I grabbed a bottle of beer and a glass of lemonade and joined him on the front porch steps. He looked refreshed and smelled divine. Priscilla, the little traitor, ran straight to him and demanded to be admired. He sat down and settled my precious Persian on his lap. "You okay, darlin'? It was a heck of day."

"I'm fine, just relieved everything ended the way it did." I watched him take a long, slow sip of beer. Really, this man was simply too handsome for his own good. It was hard to concentrate on what I wanted to say while looking at him, but that didn't mean I wanted to look away. "I've got a couple of questions for you."

His lips turned up in a slow, satisfied smile. "I've got a question for you myself."

"Me first." Heaven only knew how long I would be able to remember what I wanted to ask if he kept smiling at me like that. "How did you know where to find us? We didn't see you following us out to Walter's cabin. It's like you were magically able to track us down."

Just as I thought, he winced ever so slightly at my use of the word "track". "Guilty as charged. I confess that I used a tracking device to keep tabs on you just in case things went crazy, which they did." He gently stroked Pricilla's head. "It was wrong of me, and I believe you could bring charges against me if you saw fit."

"I would never do that." I saw that he was relieved at my words. "I know you wanted to make sure I was safe. But tell me how you did it."

"I stopped by a couple of days ago and asked Gertie if I could see the shoes you were planning to wear to the wedding. I managed to slip a tiny tracking device in the very tip of one of the toes."

My eyebrows rose. It must have been minuscule because I hadn't felt anything. "Gertie just let you see my shoes? She didn't question why?"

Kase grinned. "She questioned me, all right, and when I tried to sidestep a direct answer, she assumed I had a foot fetish. I didn't set her straight." He shrugged apologetically. "I hope that doesn't make things too awkward for you."

I waved away his concern. "Gertie believes what she wants to believe."

"You're not angry with me then?" Kase's tone was uncertain.

"How could I be? If you hadn't shown up and called for help, I don't think we could have gotten medical care for Walter in time. Several more hours in that cabin and he would have lost too much blood. So, no. I'm not mad. But I'm not thrilled either."

"Fair enough." Kase placed a hand over his heart. "I promise to be up-front with you about everything from now on."

"So, am I officially forgiven for the whole cookies and drugged milk fiasco?" When he nodded, I couldn't help but smile. A conversation like this could only take place in Sinful. "I have two more questions."

"Shoot."

"When did you start to think Lenora might be involved in the kidnapping?"

"When you told me that Fortune believed it." He saw me wrinkle my nose in response to that answer. "Think what you want, Stephanie, but her instincts are sound."

That, I didn't care to debate. Fortune was a puzzle I needed to solve, but not tonight.

"Last question. When I ran toward the cabin, what took you so long to catch up? I thought you were right behind me." I tucked a stray strand of hair behind my ear. "Did you give me time with Lenora because you thought I could talk her down? Did you trust that I could handle her?" I admit that I was looking for a yes answer to bolster my ego.

Kase shook his head. "You did great, darlin', and I'm proud of you, but the truth is that I had to head back to the truck when dispatch called with questions. I didn't want Lenora to hear the phone, or the ambulance to get lost on the way here. I felt like my own damn secretary."

I couldn't help but laugh. That wasn't the answer I expected, but I appreciated his honesty. "So, what's your question for me?"

Kase cleared his throat. "I was thinking – hoping actually – that you'd think about maybe taking a few days – well, I mean maybe you'd consider—"

I reached over, gathered up Priscilla, and unceremoniously dumped her on the top step so I could scoot closer to Kase. "I'd love to go away with you, if that's what you're trying to ask."

The twinkle in his eyes signaled his relief at not having to finish his question, as well as pleasure with my answer.

"Just don't ask me to go anywhere that involves a cabin, unless it's a cruise ship. I've seen enough of them since my arrival in Sinful to last me a lifetime. Otherwise, I'll happily go anywhere with you."

He laughed as he took my hands in his. "You're sure? Because what I have in mind isn't exactly prim and proper."

"I'm sure." I leaned in and brushed my lips across his. It was time Kase learned that I didn't need to be prim and proper. Not all the time.

A Note from Caroline

Thank you so much for taking the time to read this book. I enjoyed writing it and hope that you enjoyed reading it enough to pick up the next in my Miss Prim and Proper Series, A Sinful Mistake.
Thanks to Jana DeLeon for her generosity in sharing her Miss Fortune world with other writers!
To learn more about my other books, please visit my website -
www.carolinemickelson.com[1]
I'd love to have you join my VIP Reader Newsletter so that you can be the first to hear about new releases, discounts, and contests. Join us!

---

1. http://www.carolinemickelson.com

9 798201 248888